DOCTOR WHO
AND THE
AUTON INVASION

DOCTOR WHO
AND THE
AUTON INVASION

Based on the BBC television serial *Spearhead from Space*
by Robert Holmes by arrangement with the BBC

TERRANCE DICKS

Introduction by
RUSSELL T DAVIES

Illustrated by
Chris Achilleos

BOOKS

1 3 5 7 9 10 8 6 4 2

Published in 2011 by BBC Books, an imprint of Ebury Publishing
A Random House Group Company
First published in 1974 by Universal-Tandem Publishing Co., Ltd.

Novelisation copyright © Terrance Dicks 1974
Original script © Robert Holmes 1970
Illustrations © Chris Achilleos 1974
Introduction © Russell T Davies 2011
The Changing Face of Doctor Who and About the Authors © Justin Richards 2011
Between the Lines © Steve Tribe 2011
Autons © Estate of Robert Holmes

The Random House Group Limited Reg. No. 954009

Addresses for companies within the Random House Group can be found at
www.randomhouse.co.uk

A CIP catalogue record for this book is available from the British Library.

ISBN 978 1 849 90193 2

MIX
Paper from
responsible sources
FSC® C016897

The Random House Group Limited supports The Forest Stewardship Council
(FSC®), the leading international forest certification organisation. Our books
carrying the FSC label are printed on FSC® certified paper. FSC is the only
forest certification scheme endorsed by the leading environmental organisations,
including Greenpeace. Our paper procurement policy can be found at
www.randomhouse.co.uk/environment

Commissioning editor: Albert DePetrillo
Editorial manager: Nicholas Payne
Series consultant: Justin Richards
Project editor: Steve Tribe
Cover design: Lee Binding © Woodlands Books Ltd, 2011
Cover illustration: Chris Achilleos
Production: Rebecca Jones

Printed and bound by CPI Group (UK) Ltd, Croydon, CR0 4YY

To buy books by your favourite authors and register for offers,
visit www.randomhouse.co.uk

Contents

Russell T Davies

I met my first fellow fan through these Target books.

Of course, everyone watched *Doctor Who* in the old days, just as they do now. But as a Swansea kid in the '60s and '70s, I didn't really have a concept of fandom. *Doctor Who* was just a permanent and lovely thing, and no one could possibly be watching ITV on a Saturday night, could they? Simple as that.

But slowly, I became aware of a bigger world. Other forms of *Doctor Who*. Comic strips, the word 'Rolykin', the TV21 Daleks, and best of all, prose versions of old stories, in which things were slightly different from the programme I knew; differences that were thrilling, and mind-expanding. I'd never have called this stuff 'merchandise'. It was so much more than that! Looking back, it's easy to focus on the things we didn't have in those days – no DVD, no streaming, no Watch+1 – but maybe that vacuum made the things we did have more potent. Could a novelisation ever be so mysterious, these days? Tempting us in, with a permanent and yet askew version of the Doctor's adventures…?

It all began with *Doctor Who and the Daleks*. My neighbour, Ceri, had a copy of the paperback. Looking back, it must have been one of the first editions – the 'Armada paperback for boys and girls', before the Target range existed. Its dramatic cover haunted me. And I mean properly; I'd stare at it for ages, quite literally mesmerised. I'd ask to borrow the book and then keep it for weeks, hoping that Ceri would forget and not ask for it back. He always remembered, damn it. And so my life of crime began. One day, I just took it. Stuffed it in my pocket, smuggled it home, kept it hidden behind some other books, so only I would know it was there. And then it haunted me in a different, darker way, wedged in its shadowy hiding place; glowering and growing, like the cat in Vernon Scannell's poem, 'A Case of Murder'.

Why was it so important, to own it? I'm still not sure, though I've wondered about this for decades. But later, when I came to actually work on *Doctor Who* (you may remember me from such classics as Children In Need Cutaway and Tonight's the Night's Alien Talent Search with John Barrowman), I'd always get annoyed when cynics would dismiss merchandise as money-making. We have teams of people who fight to raise standards on the books and toys, because these things are important. For children in particular, I think, it's part of owning the show, of participating; it brings that world of imagination into your hand, into your home, into your life of breakfast, school and bed. Maybe it closes the gap between Swansea and Skaro, just a little.

So, anyway, I had my guilty paperback festering away. But then, as though the world was growing up in sync with my little self, the book range became bigger. Target came along! *Doctor Who and the Daleks* was reprinted, with a better cover! Then more books. Monthly! Books promising books-to-come in the flyleaf!

And that's when I met her. That other fan. I was in

WH Smith. Checking the *Doctor Who* shelf, as I did every week, just in case. And joy of joys, this turned out to be an incredible day – two new novelisations released at the same time! *The Daemons* and *The Sea Devils*, together!

So I reached for those two books. Just as another hand reached for those two books. And we looked at each other and laughed. Two schoolkids. She was a bit older than me, I think, standing there with her mum. We said something like, 'Me too!' 'That's funny!' Pause. 'I love these books!' 'And me!' And that was that. We went our separate ways.

There's no great punchline to that tale. Sadly, I was doomed to never marry, so it's not the romcom ending you're hoping for. But that's the point: nothing happened except something truly massive – I met someone who loved *Doctor Who* as much as I did, someone whose love went beyond a Saturday night and into that greater world of artifacts, jewels and myths. I realised I wasn't alone. And as a result, although I've forgotten terrifying amounts of my ordinary days, I have remembered that simple moment for almost 40 years.

I wonder. Who was she? Did she stay in love with *Doctor Who*? Might she even buy this edition? Oh, I wonder.

But the world moves on. The Doctor disappeared, and then came back. Idiot parents now try to take Vernon Scannell's poem off the school syllabus, in case it makes children think too hard. And Ceri asked me to autograph a *Doctor Who Annual* for his lovely daughters, last Christmas (they remembered me from such classics as Who Peter and Russell's Comic Maker Hints & Tips. Or maybe Ceri just used the girls to distract me while he searched my bedroom). But the world keeps turning round to meet itself, and now these lovely books are back.

This one's a wonder. A stone-cold classic, frankly. Written by Terrance Dicks – who should surely be Sir Terrance, for enthralling a whole generation of kids – it contains a sentence that chilled me, thirty-seven years ago, and chills me now. As the villain reveals the true extent of his plan, we are told, 'And Channing smiled a terrible smile.' I'm not kidding – it genuinely thrills me, just to type those words out, after all this time!

But that's how vital a book can be, how powerful, how forever. This is so much more than merchandise. I knew that, as a kid, and so did Ceri, and so did that unknown girl. We're a disparate little bunch of schoolkids, strangers, neighbours. But these novels are connecting us together, even now.

All the way across time and space.

The Changing Face of Doctor Who

The Third Doctor

This *Doctor Who* novel features the third incarnation of the Doctor, whose appearance was altered by his own people, the Time Lords, when they exiled him to Earth. This was his punishment for daring to steal a TARDIS, leave his homeworld and interfere in the affairs of other life forms. The Time Lords sentenced the Doctor to exile on twentieth-century Earth. The secrets of the TARDIS were taken from him and his appearance was changed.

While on Earth the Doctor formed an alliance and friendship with Brigadier Lethbridge-Stewart, head of the British branch of UNIT. Working as UNIT's Scientific Adviser, the Doctor helped the organisation to deal with all manner of threats to humanity in return for facilities to try to repair the TARDIS and a sporty, yellow Edwardian-style car he calls Bessie.

UNIT

UNIT in the United Kingdom is under the command of the ever-practical and down-to-earth Brigadier Lethbridge-Stewart. He first met the Second Doctor, and fought with him against the Yeti and the Cybermen. UNIT is a military organisation, with its headquarters in Geneva but with personnel seconded from the armed forces of each host nation. The remit of UNIT is rather vague, but according to the Brigadier, it deals with 'the odd, the unexplained. Anything on Earth, or even beyond…'

From mad scientists to alien invasions, from revived prehistoric civilisations to dinosaurs rampaging through London, UNIT has its work cut out.

Doctor Elizabeth Shaw

Doctor Elizabeth Shaw has an important research programme going ahead at Cambridge when she is invited to join UNIT. Before he encounters the Doctor again, the Brigadier has decided he needs a scientific adviser and Liz Shaw is an expert in meteorites, with degrees in 'medicine, physics, and a dozen other subjects'.

Liz is initially sceptical of the Brigadier's stories about 'little blue men with three heads…' telling him that she deals with facts, not science fiction ideas. But after meeting the Doctor – and experiencing an attempted alien invasion at first hand, she is more willing to accept the unexpected.

Prologue: Exiled to Earth

In the High Court of the Time Lords a trial was coming to its end. The accused, a renegade Time Lord known as the Doctor, had already been found guilty. Now it was time for the sentence.

The Doctor looked very out of place standing amongst the dignified Time Lords in their long white robes. To begin with, he was quite a small man. He wore an ancient black coat and a pair of check trousers. He had a gentle, rather comical face and a shock of untidy black hair. But there was strength in that face, too, and keen intelligence in the blue eyes.

A hush fell as the President of the Court rose, and began to speak. 'Doctor, you have been found guilty of two serious offences against our laws. First, you stole a TARDIS and used it to roam through Time and Space as you pleased.'

'Nonsense,' said the Doctor indignantly. 'I didn't steal it. Just borrowed it for a while.'

The President ignored the interruption. 'More important, you have repeatedly broken our most important law: interference in the affairs of other planets is a serious crime.'

Again the Doctor interrupted: 'I not only admit my interference, I am proud of it! *You* just observe the evil in the galaxies. I fight against it.'

'We have accepted your plea, Doctor, that there is evil in the Universe which must be fought. You still have a part to play in that great struggle.'

At once the Doctor began to look hopeful. 'You mean you're going to let me go?'

'Not entirely. We have noted your interest in the planet Earth. You have visited it many times. You must have special knowledge of that world and its problems.'

'I suppose I have,' agreed the Doctor.

'You will be sent to Earth in the Twentieth Century Time Zone. You will remain there for as long as we think proper. And for that time the secret of the TARDIS will be taken from you.'

The Doctor was indignant. 'You can't condemn me to exile on one primitive planet, in one particular time.'

The President's voice was cold. 'We can, and we do. That is the verdict of this Court.'

A new thought struck the Doctor. 'Besides, I'm known on Earth already. It could be most embarrassing for me.'

'Your appearance has changed before. It will change again. That is part of your sentence.'

The Doctor continued to protest. 'You can't just change what I look like without asking me!'

'You will have an opportunity to choose your new appearance,' said the President patiently. 'Look!'

As if by magic, a huge screen appeared on one wall of the Court. Upon it the Doctor saw a wide variety of faces and forms. At once the Doctor started to make trouble. He rejected each one with the utmost scorn. 'Too thin. Too fat. Too young. Too old. No, I certainly don't want to look like that, I can tell you.'

The President of the Court sighed. They were letting the

fellow off lightly. He ought to be humble and grateful, not kick up all this fuss. 'You are wasting time, Doctor,' said the President. 'Since you refuse to take the decision, we shall take it for you.'

The Doctor made no secret of his indignation.

'Well, I've got a right to decide what I'm going to look like,' he grumbled. 'They attach a great deal of importance to these things on Earth. I mean, it's not my fault if this is the best you can do, is it? I've never seen such a terrible looking bunch!'

Ignoring the Doctor's protests and complaints, the President sent a thought-impulse to a fellow Time Lord who sat at a nearby control panel. The Time Lord's fingers moved swiftly over the rows of buttons.

Immediately the Doctor was held in the grip of a force-field. Unable to move, he felt the entire courtroom dissolve round him into a sort of spinning blackness.

Sam Seeley moved through Oxley Woods like a rather tubby ghost. Sam was the most expert poacher for miles around, and proud of it. Many a time he'd slipped by within inches of a watching gamekeeper. Soundlessly he moved through the woods, stopping from time to time to check his rabbit traps.

He mopped the sweat from his brow as he moved along. No business to be as hot as this, not in October. Worse than a midsummer night it was. Seeley blamed it on those atom bombs. Suddenly a fierce whizzing and hissing filled the air around him. Terrified, Seeley dropped to the ground, muffling his head in his poacher's sack. The terrifying noise continued. He heard soft thumping sounds, as if heavy objects were burying themselves in the forest earth around him. At last there came silence.

Sam looked up cautiously. Within a few feet of his head the ground was smoking gently. Cautiously Sam reached for a stick and started to scrape away the earth. Within minutes he uncovered the top half of a buried sphere, roughly the size of a football. The sphere was smooth, almost transparent. It pulsed and glowed with an angry green light. It seemed somehow alive. Sam reached out to touch it, then pulled back his hand. The thing was red hot.

Hurriedly, Sam replaced the earth over his find and moved away. He'd come back again when it had cooled down, in daylight. He set off for home.

But Sam Seeley was in for an even more terrifying experience as he crossed the dark woods. Just as he came to a moonlit clearing, a strange wheezing and groaning filled

the air. Sam slipped behind a tree and froze as still as any rabbit.

Before his unbelieving gaze an old blue police box was appearing out of thin air. It took shape, becoming solid as he watched. The weird groaning sound died away and the box just stood there, looking sad and lost in the moonlit clearing. Slowly, the door started to open.

Not daring to move, Sam watched as a man came out of the police box. A tall thin man, with a deeply lined face and untidy white hair. Terrified as he was, Sam noticed that the man's old black coat and check trousers were both far too small for him.

The man looked around as if in a daze. He looked straight at Sam, yet didn't seem to see him. Frowning with concentration, the man produced a key and carefully looked the door of the police box behind him. Then he took a couple of wobbly steps and collapsed.

At this Sam Seeley's nerve finally broke. He crashed off through the woods, running for home like a man chased by demons.

2

The Mystery of the Meteorites

Elizabeth Shaw was very angry indeed. It didn't help a bit that the tall army officer sitting on the other side of his desk seemed to find her anger mildly amusing.

'Now see here, General,' she began angrily.

'Just "Brigadier", Miss Shaw. Brigadier Alastair Lethbridge-Stewart, at your service.'

'Since you seem to be in charge of this silly James Bond outfit—'

Again the Brigadier interrupted, this time sounding rather hurt. 'I take it you're referring to UNIT – the United Nations Intelligence Taskforce?'

'I don't care what you call yourselves. I'm just trying to make it clear to you that I'm not interested in playing secret agents with you. I happen to have a very important research programme under way at Cambridge.'

The Brigadier looked through a file on the desk in front of him. 'I'm well aware of your scientific qualifications, Miss Shaw. An expert in meteorites, degrees in physics, medicine and a dozen other subjects. Just the sort of all-rounder I've been looking for!' The Brigadier sat back, stroking his clipped moustache with an infuriatingly self-satisfied air.

Liz Shaw took a deep breath, and made a tremendous effort to control herself. 'You scoop me up from my laboratories in Cambridge, whizz me down here in a fast car, and expect me to join some ridiculous spy outfit, just like that! Why me, for Heaven's sake?'

The Brigadier said, 'We need your help, Miss Shaw. You'll find the laboratory facilities here are really first class.'

'And what am I supposed to do with them? Invent a better kind of invisible ink?'

'I think you have rather a mistaken idea of our work here at UNIT. We're not exactly spies, you know. If I could explain?'

Liz realised that, in spite of her anger, she was really rather curious about what was going on. 'All right,' she said. 'Just what do you do – exactly?'

The Brigadier paused for a moment, obviously choosing his words with great care. 'We deal with the odd – the unexplained. We're prepared to tackle anything on Earth. Or even from beyond the Earth, if necessary.'

Liz looked at him in amazement. To her astonishment he seemed quite serious. 'You mean alien invaders?' she said incredulously. 'Little blue men from Mars with three heads?'

'Early this morning,' said the Brigadier, 'a shower of about fifty meteorites landed in Essex.'

Liz's scientific curiosity was aroused at once. 'Landed? Most meteorites don't even reach the Earth's surface. They burn up in the atmosphere.'

The Brigadier nodded. 'Exactly. But these didn't.'

'Were they exceptionally large?'

'Rather small if anything. And they came down through a funnel of thin, super-heated air twenty miles in diameter – for which no one has been able to provide an explanation.'

Liz frowned. 'Some kind of freak heat-wave?'

'Perhaps. But the temperature in that area was over

8

twenty-eight Centigrade. A few miles away there was ground-frost.'

'There must *be* an explanation,' said Liz thoughtfully. 'A natural one, I mean.' She didn't sound very convincing, even to herself.

'I hope there is. I've cordoned off the area and I've got men searching now. But we didn't find anything last time.'

Liz looked up sharply. 'Last time?'

Grimly the Brigadier nodded. 'Six months ago, a smaller shower of meteorites, five or six of them, landed in the same area.'

'That's impossible!' said Liz. 'The odds against two lots of meteorites landing in the same place must be enormous.'

With some satisfaction the Brigadier looked at the girl in front of his desk. At last she was beginning to realise the true seriousness of the situation.

Liz went on: 'In fact the odds are so high as to be scientifically unacceptable.' She stood up and paced about the office, thinking aloud. 'So if we rule out coincidence, there can be only one other explanation. Those meteorites – both showers – must have been…' Her voice tailed off as she couldn't bring herself to say the final words.

The Brigadier finished the sentence for her. 'That's right. The meteorite swarms must have been directed. Deliberately aimed at this planet.'

In the reception hall of Ashbridge Cottage Hospital Captain Munro, of UNIT, was arguing with an irate casualty officer. Fortunately, Munro, a dark-haired, smoothly handsome young man, was something of a diplomat. He was used to smoothing down awkward civilians, and he answered all Doctor Henderson's objections with infuriating politeness.

In the background, two soldiers, Regular Army men on attachment to UNIT, waited patiently, carrying between them a stretcher on which lay a still, blanket-covered form.

'Dammit man,' said Doctor Henderson crossly, 'why didn't you take him to a military hospital?'

Munro sighed. 'For one thing, sir, there isn't one in the area. And for another…' Munro turned to the stretcher and pulled back the blanket. 'As you can see, the chap's obviously a civilian.'

Henderson looked in amazement at the tall, thin figure on the stretcher. Coat and trousers were both far too small, leaving bony wrists and ankles stretching out in a scarecrow fashion. 'Not a very military figure, I agree,' admitted Doctor Henderson. 'All right, I suppose I'd better take a look at him.' He turned to the soldiers carrying the stretcher. 'Take him through into Casualty, will you? The porter will show you the way.' At a nod from Munro, the soldiers carried the stretcher through the swing-doors into the casualty ward.

'You've no idea who he is, I suppose?' asked Henderson. Munro shook his head. 'Haven't a clue, sir. There's no identification on him, I'm afraid.'

Henderson heaved a sigh. 'You don't realise the amount of paperwork these cases involve,' he said wearily. 'Reports to the police, memos to the Hospital Committee. All in triplicate.'

Like any good soldier, Captain Munro knew when it was time to beat a retreat. 'You really have been awfully good sir,' he said smoothly. 'I'm sure the Brigadier will be most grateful.' Munro looked at his watch. 'Which reminds me, I really ought to 'phone in a report. I wonder if I might…'

'Over there,' said Henderson, nodding towards a

'phone booth in the corner. 'Mind you, this chap's still your responsibility.'

Munro didn't commit himself. 'Thanks again, sir,' he said with his most charming smile. 'Now, if you'll excuse me...'

Hastily Munro disappeared inside the 'phone booth. Henderson, realising he'd been out-manoeuvred, turned and went through the swing-doors after his new patient.

Back at UNIT H.Q., Brigadier Lethbridge-Stewart was still trying to persuade Liz Shaw to accept the unbelievable.

'Don't you see, Miss Shaw, it's just *because* everyone takes your attitude, refuses to believe the evidence, that the Earth is in so much danger.'

'Why is Earth any more likely to be attacked now than at any time during the last fifty thousand years?' said Liz obstinately.

'Isn't that obvious? Space probes, rocket launches, men on the moon...' The Brigadier leaned forward, his voice urgent. 'We have drawn attention to ourselves, Miss Shaw.'

Liz sank back into her chair. 'I'm sorry,' she said, 'but I just can't swallow it. I admit I've got no explanation for your meteor swarms – but invasion from outer space!'

For a moment the Brigadier was silent, then he seemed to come to a decision. 'And if I were to tell you that to my personal knowledge there have been two attempts to conquer the planet Earth, both by intelligent life forms from beyond this galaxy?'

All Liz could do was stare at him open-mouthed. He's cracking up, she thought wildly. Over-work probably. Been reading too much science-fiction. The Brigadier was still talking, quietly and calmly, apparently very much in control of his wits.

'UNIT was formed as a direct result of the first attempt. And I am proud to say that it played a very large part in preventing the second invasion.'

'Well done,' said Liz faintly. She wondered if she ought to start heading towards the door, before the Brigadier suddenly decided she was a Martian spy.

The Brigadier seemed lost in his memories. 'Though, of course, we weren't alone. We had help. Very valuable help.' He looked up and smiled. 'To be perfectly honest, Miss Shaw, you weren't my first choice for the post of UNIT'S Scientific Adviser.'

Despite herself, Liz felt a bit resentful. 'Oh? And who was then?'

'A man called "the Doctor",' answered the Brigadier.

'Doctor?' said Liz. 'Doctor who?'

The Brigadier chuckled. 'Who indeed? I don't think he ever told us his name. But he was the most brilliant scientist I have ever met. No disrespect, Miss Shaw.'

'So why didn't you get this mysterious genius to be your Scientific Adviser, instead of practically kidnapping me?'

'Don't think I didn't try,' said the Brigadier ruefully. 'Unfortunately, he tends to appear and disappear as he pleases. I tried to get hold of him when they decided we needed a resident scientist. The Intelligence services of the entire world were unable to turn up any trace of him.'

'So you decided to make do with me?'

'And a great success you'll make of it, I'm sure,' said the Brigadier. Liz couldn't help smiling at the compliment. Despite his stiff military manner, there was something very likable about the Brigadier.

The 'phone on the Brigadier's desk buzzed, and with a gesture of apology to Liz the Brigadier picked it up.

12

'Munro here, sir,' said the voice at the other end. 'I'm at the Ashbridge Cottage Hospital.'

'Have you found any trace of those meteorites?'

'No sir. All we've found so far is one unconscious civvie. I've just turned him over to the local hospital.'

'Captain Munro,' said the Brigadier acidly, 'if you've nothing better to report than the finding of a drunken tramp sleeping it off in the woods, I suggest you get off the 'phone and get on with the search.'

'The chap wasn't drunk sir. Half-dead more like it. And I don't think it was a tramp. Weirdest thing you ever saw, sir. A police box slap in the middle of the woods, and this fellow lying spark-out beside it.'

'A police box?' said the Brigadier. 'You did say a *police box*?' His voice was suddenly eager and excited.

'That's right, sir,' said Munro cheerfully. 'Suppose I ought to tell the police, really. I mean they may want the thing back.'

The Brigadier's voice was brisk. 'On no account, Munro. I want an armed guard on that police box right away. Nobody's to be allowed near it. Nobody! Is that clear?'

'Yes sir,' said Munro automatically. 'But I don't quite understand, sir…'

The Brigadier's voice cut in. 'This man you found. You say he's at the hospital?'

'In Casualty now sir. The Doctor's taking a look at him. The man seems to be in a sort of a coma.'

'Right,' said the Brigadier crisply. 'Armed guard on him too, Munro. Nobody's to talk to him till I arrive.'

'Very good sir,' said Munro, by now thoroughly puzzled.

'I'll come down right away. Oh – and Munro, I'll be

bringing our new Scientific Adviser with me. Meanwhile, keep the patrols searching.'

The Brigadier slammed down the 'phone and sat for a moment lost in thought. 'It can't be,' he said, almost to himself. 'But a police box! And it would be just like him, turning up like that out of the blue.'

'Just like who?' said Liz, now thoroughly curious.

The Brigadier grinned. 'Come and see for yourself. I'd like you to come down to Essex with me right away.'

'But why? What's going on?'

'That,' said the Brigadier, 'is exactly what I hope to find out. If my chaps do turn up any of these meteorites you'll be able to do an on-the-spot examination. And I want to see this man they've found for myself. Shall we go?'

Liz Shaw hesitated for a moment. She realised that this was her last chance to insist on her rights, to refuse the ridiculous hush-hush job she was being offered and return to the quiet, sane, sensible world of scientific research.

'Shall we go, Miss Shaw?' repeated the Brigadier.

Liz looked at him and saw the appeal behind the formal manner. Suddenly she realised that the Brigadier really was worried, that he really did need her help. Why me, she thought, why me? There must be heaps of people better qualified.

But she also realised that she was now much too caught up in this mysterious business of invading alien forces, intelligent meteorites and mysterious men with police boxes, to draw back now. If she did, she'd be torn with curiosity for the rest of her life. She got up and strode to the door which the Brigadier was holding open for her. 'Come along then, Brigadier,' she said briskly, 'what are we wasting time for?'

14

The Brigadier stood astonished as Liz strode past him and marched off down the corridor. Then, deciding not for the first time that he would never understand the ways of women, he hurried after her.

3

The Man from Space

In a small private room, Ashbridge Cottage Hospital's latest arrival lay motionless on the bed. Henderson stood over him, his face a picture of astonishment. He'd expected all along that the new arrival would mean trouble. But not this kind of trouble. Hovering as it seemed between life and death, the new patient was showing reflexes and reactions that Henderson had never encountered before.

Henderson looked up eagerly as a nurse entered with a batch of X-ray plates. Surely these would throw some light on things. The nurse looked at the still figure on the bed. 'How is he, Doctor?'

Henderson turned away to look at the X-rays. 'I only wish I knew,' he said honestly. The nurse leaned over the patient, automatically smoothing the pillows and straightening the sheets. The man on the bed was quiet and still, scarcely breathing. She studied the still features for a moment. It was a strange face. Sometimes it seemed handsome and dignified, sometimes quizzical, almost comic. The seams and wrinkles, the shock of almost white hair should have made it an old face, yet somehow there was a strong impression of energy and youth.

Suddenly the nurse drew back in amazement as two very blue eyes flicked open, and studied her with interest. Then solemnly one of them winked. Both eyes closed and the man seemed to subside into his coma.

'Nurse!' Henderson's voice made her jump. It was cold with anger. 'Would you mind coming over here, please?'

The nurse trembled. Like all the other nurses in the hospital, she was terrified of Henderson and his sharp tongue. What could be wrong now, she thought. Maybe those idiots in radiology had sent up the wrong plates. Whatever it was, she'd be the one to get the blame. Inwardly quaking, she crossed to where Henderson was examining the X-rays on a lighted stand. 'Is there anything wrong, Doctor?' she said, trying to keep her voice calm.

Henderson pointed to the X-ray. 'You have, I take it, studied the human anatomy as part of your training?'

The nurse sighed. 'Of course, Doctor.'

Henderson jabbed a quivering finger at the X-ray plate. 'Then perhaps you would be kind enough to tell me what that is?'

She followed the direction of the finger. 'It's the patient's heart, Doctor.'

Henderson's finger moved across to the other side of the plate. 'Then what's this, then, eh? What's this?' By now he was so angry that his voice came out only as a sort of strangulated shriek.

The nurse, now completely terrorised, leaned forward and peered nervously at the X-ray. Then she drew a deep breath. 'It appears to be another heart, sir.'

'Exactly,' said Henderson grimly. 'Another heart. And that, as we know, is impossible, isn't it, nurse? Now then, which of your jolly medical student friends is responsible for this little prank, eh?'

The nurse struggled to control her quavering voice. 'I don't know, Doctor, honestly. All I did was wait till the plates were ready and bring them back to you.'

Henderson studied her narrowly and saw that she was much too terrified to be relating anything except the truth. As always, he regretted his quick temper. 'All right,' he said gruffly, 'probably wasn't your fault. But someone in that X-ray Department is playing games with me, and I'm going to find out who it is.' He was about to stride from the room when the internal 'phone bleeped. The nurse picked it up. An angry voice said in her ear: 'This is Lomax. Pathology Lab. Is Doctor Henderson there?'

The nurse almost dropped the 'phone from pure terror. If there was anyone more feared than Doctor Henderson, it was old Doctor Lomax in Pathology. Silently she handed the 'phone to Doctor Henderson. He took it and said, 'Doctor Henderson. Well?'

The fierce Scottish voice jabbed at his eardrums. 'No, Doctor Henderson, it's no' well at all. Not when ye've the time to play wee stupid tricks on a busy man like me.'

Henderson's bad temper returned full blast. He and Lomax were old enemies. 'What the blazes are you talking about?'

'I am talking, Doctor Henderson, about the sample of blood ye've just sent us for cross matching. Ye admit ye sent the sample?'

'Of course I did. It's routine. You know that. What's the matter with it?'

The voice on the 'phone was airily sarcastic. 'Oh nothing, Doctor Henderson, nothing. Except that it's not human blood, as you very well know.'

Henderson said angrily. 'What do you mean, not human? I took it from the patient myself.'

'It is not human blood,' said Lomax emphatically. 'The

19

platelet stickiness is quite different and it corresponds to no known human blood-type.'

'Now you listen to me, Doctor Lomax. I took that blood sample from an adult male patient who is lying on the bed in front of me now. You tell me it's not human. His X-ray tells me he's got two hearts. Now I don't know whether that makes me a doctor, a vet or a raving lunatic, but as far as I'm concerned those are the facts.'

Henderson slammed down the 'phone, feeling considerably better for his outburst. He turned to the nurse, who braced herself for another blast, and was astonished when Henderson said gently, 'It seems I owe you an apology, nurse.' He crossed to the bed and looked down at the sleeping man. 'Well, whoever or whatever you are, old chap, you're still a patient, and it's my job to look after you.' Henderson turned to the nurse with a worried smile. 'The only thing is – I haven't the faintest idea where to start.'

They both looked down at the man on the bed. The nurse said, 'I thought he was coming round a moment ago, but he seems to have…'

She stopped as the man on the bed opened his eyes again. This time he was frowning. He said clearly, 'My lord, I wish to protest in the strongest terms… the sentence is… I insist on my rights…'

The voice tailed away and the patient slept again. In the corridor outside, Mullins, the hospital porter, abandoned a half-mopped floor and moved off towards the foyer. No one paid Mullins any attention as he slipped across the foyer and into the 'phone booth. He was a seedy little man, easy to ignore. Quickly he dialled the local paper, hands trembling with excitement. In a moment he was speaking to one of the junior reporters.

'Listen, I've got something for you.'

In a clump of bushes at the edge of Oxley Woods, Sam Seeley crouched as motionless as one of the rabbits he had so often poached. In the distance he could hear the crashing of heavily booted feet, the sound of shouted orders as the army patrols called to each other on their search.

With military precision the soldiers had divided the woods into sections, and were methodically combing them, one by one. The woods were thick and dark, the ground between the trees heavily overgrown with gorse and bracken. The search was taking a long time. So far they had found nothing. They certainly hadn't found Sam Seeley, who slipped through the patrols at will, sometimes passing within a few feet of them.

The sounds of search came nearer. Sam peered through a gap in the bushes and saw a three-man patrol approaching. Two of the soldiers were carrying some kind of mine-detector, while the third, a corporal, was directing their search. Sam grinned to himself. He knew what they were looking for. What's more, he knew where to find it.

After his terrifying experience in the woods, the previous night, Sam had been glad to slip back to his little cottage and creep into bed. His wife, Meg, pretended to be asleep as he crept into bed beside her. She knew well enough where he'd been, but preferred not to show it. Although she would never admit that Sam was a poacher, she'd no objection to the plump rabbits or partridges that appeared on the kitchen table from time to time, some to go into her stewpot, some to be sold by Sam down at the village pub.

Sam had been tossing and turning in bed, thinking over the things he'd seen. The glowing green sphere of the meteorite, the man who'd appeared by magic. Who should he tell? Above all, how could he turn a profit out of it all?

He had been wakened from an uneasy sleep just a few hours after dawn by the rumble of lorries past his window. Slipping out of bed and drawing back the curtain, he had seen the troops go by, lorry-load after lorry-load of grim silent men, clutching rifles.

As he crouched in the bushes, watching the patrol move away past him, Sam became more and more convinced that he was doing the right thing. Anything that was worth so much trouble must also be worth a lot of money. Let the soldier boys crash round the woods as much as they liked. Then, when they were desperate, they'd be ready to pay and pay well for the thing he'd found. Some piece of Government equipment, he reckoned. Something they'd shot up in the air that hadn't come down where it was meant to. Well, they could have their nice green ball back. But not for nothing. Meanwhile he'd better get his find to a safe place, just in case one of those soldiers happened to get lucky. The patrol was almost out of sight now. Sam slipped into the woods, making for the clearing where he'd found the glowing ball. This time there was a shovel and a sheet of the wife's new-fangled kitchen foil in the sack he carried.

Retracing his steps of last night, Sam skirted the edge of the clearing where the strange blue box had appeared. The man had gone but the box was still there. Now, in the daylight, he could see that it was nothing more than an old blue police box. A sentry stood guarding it. He was young and nervous looking. In his curiosity Sam forgot to watch his footing and stepped into a crackly patch of dry bracken. Immediately the sentry's rifle swung round.

'Halt. Who goes there? Answer, or I fire!' Sam dropped

to the ground and froze. The sentry's voice was high-pitched with nerves. The sentry swung his rifle around, covering the thick forest. Except for some distant bird song, the silence was complete. Shaking his head at his own nervousness, the sentry shouldered his rifle, went back to guarding the police box. How much longer were they going to leave him here, anyway? What was the point of guarding a police box that some idiot had stolen and carried out here?

In the trees, Sam heaved a sigh of relief and slipped away. After a narrow shave with another patrol – the soldier was having a crafty doze and Sam almost stepped on him – he found himself back in the part of the woods where he'd made his find. To most people that bit of wood looked like any other, but to Sam it was as easily identifiable as if

there'd been street names and signposts. That oddly shaped branch there, that little fold of land there, little thorn bush here… Sam lined up his landmarks, produced his spade and began to dig.

In a few moments the blade of the shovel touched something hard and smooth. Sam began to dig cautiously round the sphere. Whatever it was, he didn't want to damage it. Soon the green globe was fully uncovered. It still pulsated, but it seemed quieter, more subdued, in the daylight. Sam reached out and touched it cautiously. Still warm, but none of the searing heat of the night before. He produced his sheet of kitchen foil and began to wrap up his find.

In the hospital bed the mysterious new patient stirred. His eyes shot open. Suddenly he sat bolt upright in the bed, looking keenly around him. Apart from himself, the room was empty. He frowned and rubbed his chin as if he'd forgotten something very important. Suddenly he lurched forward, face down across the bed, and began to grope underneath it. It was in this position that the nurse found him when she re-entered the room.

Shocked, she rushed forward, grabbed him by the shoulders and pushed him back onto the bed.

'You really mustn't, you know,' she said firmly. 'You're not strong enough to get up yet.'

The patient struggled feebly, but it was no use. 'Shoes,' he said with sudden clarity, 'must find my shoes.'

The nurse ignored him. With professional skill she settled him back into the bed and tucked him in. 'You don't need your shoes,' she said brightly, 'because you're not going anywhere. Now try to rest.'

The man on the bed regarded her with evident disgust. 'Madam,' he said with old-fashioned politeness, 'I really must ask you… must ask you…' The voice became faint and he sank back into sleep.

The nurse was smoothing his pillows and straightening the coverlet as Doctor Henderson entered. 'Any change?'

'He recovered consciousness, Doctor, just for a few minutes. He tried to get up but I managed to calm him.'

'Did he say anything?'

'Not really. He seemed to be worried about his shoes.'

Henderson shook his head as he looked down at the patient. The man was sleeping calmly now, though a faint frown still wrinkled his forehead. 'Probably still irrational, poor chap. Well, some bigwig from UNIT's coming down to see him. Perhaps he'll know what to make of you,' said Henderson to the sleeping man, 'because I'm blowed if I do.'

At this particular moment the bigwig from UNIT, accompanied by a rather amused Liz Shaw, was trying to push his way politely but firmly through a crowd of eagerly inquisitive newspapermen and photographers in the hospital entrance hall. The Brigadier's moustache twitched with disgust as a particularly keen photographer shot off a flash-bulb right under his nose. As the leader of a supposedly secret organisation, the Brigadier felt it was all wrong to be photographed for the newspapers, and he had no idea how all these people had turned up. He only knew that they *were* there, and he very much wished that they weren't.

A tall man pushed his way to the front of the crowd. 'Wagstaffe, sir, Defence Correspondent of *The Daily Post*.'

A second reporter cut in – 'Can you give us a statement, sir?'

The Brigadier's tone was not encouraging. 'What about?'

Wagstaffe was courteous, but persistent. 'What's UNIT doing down here, sir? Is it true you've got some kind of man from space in there?'

'Nonsense,' said the Brigadier firmly. 'I don't know where you chaps get these stories from.'

'Can we have some pictures of him, sir?' said the photographer, getting another quick shot of the Brigadier meanwhile.

'Certainly not.'

'Why not, sir? Can we tell the readers they'd be too horrible to publish?' said one of the reporters hopefully. 'Have you got some kind of monster in there, sir?'

'Ridiculous,' said the Brigadier, 'I assure you there is no monster and no story for you, either, so you might as well go home.'

Wagstaffe returned to the attack. 'Then why are you here, sir? Why have your men cordoned off the whole of Oxley Woods? What are they searching for?' The questions came thick and fast now, from all the others. 'What about the freak heat-wave last night?' 'And the meteorite shower. Is there some connection?' 'What about this man from space? Is it true he's not really human?' 'Where did you find him? Have you found his space-ship yet?' 'Who's the young lady, sir? Has she come to identify the man?'

It was many years since the Brigadier had been on a barrack square, but his voice could still carry the arresting sharpness of command.

'One moment, gentlemen, *if* you please!' A rather

startled silence fell. The Brigadier looked round. Beneath his assured exterior his mind was frantically searching for a plausible story. Oddly enough, he hit upon the same idea that Sam Seeley had worked out for himself in the woods. 'All I can tell you at the moment is this. Last night some top secret Government equipment, something to do with the space programme, descended off-course and landed in this area. My men are searching for the fragments, if any, now.' Pretty convincing, that, thought the Brigadier, might almost be true. He gave himself a mental pat on the back. Indicating Liz Shaw, he said, 'This is our Scientific Adviser. She's come to help identify anything we turn up.'

'Then what about this mystery man in there?' Wagstaffe again, not to be easily put off.

The Brigadier thought fast. 'In there, gentlemen, is some unfortunate civilian who was found unconscious in the woods early this morning. We hope he may have seen the device land. He may even be able to tell us where it is.'

'And that's really all there is to it, sir?'

'That's all I can tell at the moment,' said the Brigadier rather neatly avoiding a direct lie. 'Now if you'll excuse me?'

He strode through the swing-doors into Casualty, Liz Shaw following behind. The Brigadier would have been less pleased with himself if he could have known that his flight-of-fancy had endangered the life of the man he had come to see.

As the Brigadier was beginning his explanation, a man had entered unobserved. He was standing now at the back of the crowd. The man was middle-aged, immaculately dressed, with regular, handsome features. He might have been a distinguished surgeon, or a wealthy visitor for one of the hospital patients.

One of the reporters glanced casually at him, wondering who he was. Then the reporter looked again. There was something about this man, something odd. The clothes were too immaculate, the handsome features too calm and regular. He looks like a wax dummy, thought the reporter uneasily. Like a waxwork come to life.

Sensing that he was being stared at, the new arrival looked up. The reporter recoiled physically, as if struck by a sudden blow. The stranger's eyes were staring at him, fiercely alive, almost glowing with the light of an intelligence that seemed somehow – alien. Those eyes scorched the reporter for a moment, then the man turned away, strode across the foyer, making as if to follow the Brigadier.

Mullins, the hospital porter, rather aghast at the results of his 'phone call, had been placed on guard by the door. He was being extra efficient, as if trying to make up for his previous indiscretion. As the stranger tried to follow the Brigadier, Mullins barred his way. 'Can't go in there sir, sorry. No one allowed in there at all.' The stranger raised those burning eyes and Mullins too, recoiled. But he stood firm.

'No use you glaring at me like that, mate,' he said, his voice quavering a little. 'You can't go in there and that's that. You want me to call the soldiers?'

Much to Mullins' relief the man turned on his heel and strode swiftly away, making for the telephone in the corner.

Mullins mopped his brow and swore that he'd never call the papers again.

The stranger stepped beneath the acoustic hood and stood motionless. There was no expression on the blank

28

face. The burning eyes stared into the distance, the head was cocked a little as if listening. The smooth white hands made no move to pick up the 'phone. The man simply stood there, completely motionless. Like a waxwork…

4

The Faceless Kidnappers

Brigadier Lethbridge-Stewart strode along the hospital corridor, Liz Shaw struggling to keep up with him. Captain Munro came hurriedly to meet him.

'Where the blazes did that lot come from?' snapped the Brigadier, gesturing behind him.

'No idea sir,' said Munro. 'They just appeared like swallows in the spring.' He looked enquiringly at Liz, who gave him a friendly smile.

The Brigadier grunted. 'Miss Shaw, this is Jimmy Munro, my number two.' Munro nodded a greeting and fell into step beside them.

'Got that police box under guard?' said the Brigadier.

'Yes sir. The sentry's got orders to let no one near it.'

'This man we're going to see,' said Liz. 'I gather you think he may be your mysterious Doctor?'

'I'm certain of it, Miss Shaw.'

'Why? Because of the police box?'

'Just so,' said the Brigadier. 'Because of the police box.'

'Here we are, sir,' said Munro. 'They've put him in a private room.' A sentry was guarding the door. The Brigadier acknowledged his salute and strode into the room.

Doctor Henderson stood waiting by his bed. Nothing could be seen of the bed's occupant, who had wriggled down under the covers. Briefly Munro made the necessary introductions.

'I understand you may be able to cast some light on our mystery man, Brigadier?' said Henderson. The Brigadier nodded. 'In that case,' Henderson went on, 'I'd be very grateful for some explanation of his physical make-up.'

Liz looked puzzled. 'How do you mean?'

'His whole cardio-vascular system is different from anything I've ever encountered. He appears to have *two* hearts. Moreover, his blood belongs to no known human type.'

Lethbridge-Stewart nodded, obviously delighted by this news. 'Splendid. That sounds exactly like the Doctor.' He peered at the little that could be seen of the patient. 'Hair was black, though, as I remember. Could be shock, I suppose.'

Cautiously the Brigadier drew back the sheet from the face of the man on the bed. He peered for a moment, then straightened up, his face a study in disappointment.

Liz said, 'Well? *Do* you know him?'

The Brigadier shook his head sadly. 'The man's a complete stranger.'

'You're sure?' asked Henderson.

'Of course I'm sure.' Disappointment made the Brigadier speak sharply. He looked down again at the sleeper. 'Never seen the feller before in my life.'

The eyes of the man on the bed opened wide, staring straight at the Brigadier. A sudden charming smile spread over his face.

'Lethbridge-Stewart, my dear fellow. How nice to see you again!'

'You may not know him, sir,' said Munro, 'but he seems to know you all right.'

32

Baffled, the Brigadier stared at the patient, who seemed to be drifting off to sleep again.

'But he can't do. It's impossible.' The Brigadier bent over the bed and prodded the sleeper awake.

'Steady on, Brigadier,' protested Doctor Henderson. 'He's still very weak, you know.'

But the Brigadier ignored him. 'Look here, my man, can you hear me? Who are you?'

The man opened his eyes indignantly. 'Don't be silly, my dear chap. You know who I am. I'm the Doctor.'

'You most certainly are not!'

'Come, come now, old chap. Remember the Yeti? And the Cybermen? You can't have forgotten already.' And struggling to a sitting position, the Doctor looked at his old friend in astonishment. 'Don't you recognise me?' he asked plaintively.

'I am quite positive that we have never met before.'

The Doctor passed his hand over his face in puzzlement. It didn't feel right. 'Oh dear,' he said. 'You really are sure? I can't have changed that much.' He seemed to brace himself, then asked, 'I wonder if I might borrow a mirror?'

At a nod from the Brigadier, Henderson produced a mirror from the bedside locker and handed it over. The Doctor looked into it. The face of a stranger was looking back at him.

The Doctor's mind reeled under the sudden shock. Fragments of the recent past flashed disjointedly before his eyes. His capture by the Time Lords. The trial. The faces of Jamie and Zoe as they said goodbye. The Doctor looked round him wildly. He saw the young army officer, the girl, the doctor, Lethbridge-Stewart peering at him suspiciously. Suddenly their faces began to spin round him, like the faces they'd offered him to choose from at the trial. He made an unsuccessful attempt to stand up, then collapsed backwards upon the bed.

The Brigadier made an attempt to re-awaken him, but Henderson stepped firmly between them.

'Whoever or whatever this man is, Brigadier, he's still my patient. He's tired and weak and he needs rest.'

The Brigadier rubbed his chin. 'Extraordinary business. Quite extraordinary.' He came to a decision. 'When will this man be well enough to travel?'

Henderson shrugged. 'Hard to say at the moment.'

The Brigadier turned to Munro. 'As soon as he's well enough, I want him transferred to the sick-bay at UNIT H.Q. Meanwhile, carry on with the search!'

'Very good, sir,' said Munro. They moved away from the bed.

'And keep that police box under guard. I'll send a lorry with some lifting tackle down to bring it back to H.Q.' The Brigadier looked again at the man on the bed and shook his head. 'I don't know why this chap should choose to impersonate the Doctor. But I intend to find out.'

'Er – yes, sir. Quite, sir,' said Munro, who was now completely baffled.

The Brigadier turned to the equally puzzled Liz. 'My apologies, Miss Shaw, we seem to have had a wasted journey. Doctor Henderson, is there another way out of this building?'

Henderson looked up from his patient. 'Turn left instead of right and you can get out through the kitchens.'

'Thank you, Doctor Henderson. I'll be in touch. Miss Shaw, Captain Munro.' The Brigadier strode briskly from the room, Liz and Munro following. Liz didn't resent the brusqueness of his tone. She sensed just how disappointed the Brigadier had been by his failure to meet his old friend, the Doctor.

In the entrance hall of the hospital, things were very much calmer. Most of the pressmen had gone, accepting the Brigadier's statement and making the best of it. Mislaid Government space equipment wasn't as good a story as a monster from Mars, but it was better than nothing. Only Wagstaffe was still hanging about and he wasn't quite sure himself why he bothered.

Suddenly he heard the sound of a car. He reached the hospital steps just in time to see the UNIT car drawing away. If the Brigadier's got nothing to hide, why is he sneaking out the back way, thought Wagstaffe irritably. He wandered across to the door to Casualty, where Mullins was still on guard. 'Any chance of a word with Doctor Henderson?'

Mullins shook his head. 'No use asking me. You can wait if you like.'

'Never mind. I'll ring the office and then get back.' He was moving towards the 'phone when Mullins' voice stopped him.

'Somebody's there. Been there ages, he has.'

Wagstaffe looked across to the booth. Beneath the hood he could see the figure of a man standing motionless.

'Know who he is, do you?' asked Mullins. 'Funny bloke. Eyes that go right through you.'

Wagstaffe shook his head. 'Never seen him before. He's not one of the regular boys. You say he's been there quite a while?'

Mullins nodded. 'Ever since that Brigadier came through.'

Wagstaffe moved towards the 'phone booth. 'Better winkle him out, then, hadn't we?'

'Rather you than me,' said Mullins.

Wagstaffe crossed to the booth and tapped his arm.

'Think you could get a move on, old chap?' he said pleasantly. 'You see I've got a rather urgent story to 'phone in and…'

His voice tailed away as the man in the booth swung round on him. Like Mullins before him, Wagstaffe recoiled from the fierce impact of those glaring eyes. He tried to go on.

'I mean, you have been in there quite a while and…' The man in the booth brushed past him, walked across the entrance hall and disappeared through the exit doors.

Wagstaffe looked at the telephone. It was still on its rest. He hadn't been using the 'phone at all, he thought. All that

time he had just been standing there. Like a waxwork.

'Shoes,' said the Doctor feebly. 'It's most important. Must have my shoes.'

The nurse smiled placidly as she took his pulse.

'I've already told you,' she said, as if to a child, 'you don't need your shoes because you're not going anywhere.'

That's all you know, thought the Doctor to himself. He slumped back on the pillows as Doctor Henderson entered.

'How is he, nurse?'

'He seems well enough, Doctor. But his pulse is pretty peculiar.' She handed Henderson the graph. He studied it gloomily.

'Ten a minute! Still, for all we know that might be normal for him. Heartbeat?'

'Strong and steady, sir. Both of them.'

Henderson sighed and bent over the Doctor. He spoke with professional cheerfulness. 'Hullo, old chap. How are we feeling now?'

'Shoes,' said the Doctor again.

Henderson turned to the nurse. 'Poor chap's mind seems to be wandering.'

'He seems to be worried about his shoes. I think he believes they've been stolen.'

'Well, if he's worried about them, he'd better have 'em. Might as well humour the poor fellow.'

The nurse fished under the bed and produced a rather battered pair of elastic-sided boots. Immediately, the Doctor reached forward, snatched them from her and clasped them protectively to his chest. He sank back on the bed, a blissful smile on his face, and seemed to go to sleep.

Henderson gave him a worried look. 'I wonder if there's any brain damage. I'll run some tests on him as soon as he comes out of it.'

The nurse looked at her peculiar patient. 'He's certainly been acting very erratically.'

Henderson frowned. 'Think I'll test his blood pressure while I'm here. Get the apparatus, will you please, nurse?'

As the nurse left the room Henderson checked the charts on the end of the Doctor's bed, shaking his head in sheer disbelief. How could you treat a patient whose anatomy seemed to contradict all the known laws of medicine? Those incredible X-rays!

On the bed, the Doctor opened his eyes cautiously. Henderson, brooding over the papers, was turned away from him. The Doctor up-ended his shoes, first one, then the other. From the second there dropped a key. With a sigh of relief, the Doctor closed his eyes, the key clasped tightly in his hand.

For a minute or two the little room was silent. The Doctor seemed to doze. Henderson was immersed in the charts. Neither of them seemed to notice when two men, one of them pushing a wheel-chair, slipped silently into the room.

Henderson, vaguely aware that someone was there, glanced up absently, expecting to see his returning nurse. He drew back in horror at the sight of a giant figure looming over him. He opened his mouth to shout, but an enormous hand swatted him to the floor as easily as if he had been a fly. A second before he sank into unconsciousness, Doctor Henderson noticed something peculiarly horrible about that hand. It was completely smooth and white, and *there were no fingernails.*

The two huge figures moved swiftly and efficiently. The Doctor was hoisted effortlessly into the wheel-chair. Surgical tape was slapped as a gag over his mouth. A blanket from the bed was bundled round his night-shirted form and he was wheeled from the room. The entire kidnapping had taken place in a matter of seconds. On the floor, Henderson groaned and stirred, struggling slowly to his feet. Feebly he shouted for help.

The two massive figures pushed the wheel-chair with its silent burden along the corridor. By a side door a man stood waiting. He was immaculately dressed, with handsome regular features. He stood completely still, like a waxwork. The only alive thing about him was his fiercely glowing, burning eyes.

As the two giants with the wheel-chair appeared, he opened a small side door leading to a yard. The two men wheeled the chair through the doorway and the third man hurried after them into the hospital yard.

The little party moved swiftly and silently round the corner. At the top of the steep hospital drive stood a small plain van, the back doors already open. The Doctor in his wheel-chair was pushed rapidly up to the van.

Suddenly the Doctor sprang into life. Gripping the sides of the wheel-chair, he gave a tremendous shove with both feet against the back of the van. The wheel-chair shot rapidly between the two kidnappers and landed backwards in a hedge. Adroitly the Doctor spun it round, and with another tremendous shove launched himself down the steep hospital drive. Gathering speed, he raced down the drive at a tremendous rate.

His kidnappers made as if to follow him, then at a sign from their leader leaped into the van. The leader took the

wheel and started turning the van in order to pursue the Doctor.

Doctor Henderson staggered through the hospital foyer, ignoring the astonished receptionist and reeled out onto the steps. He called hoarsely, 'There they are. Stop them! Stop them!'

At this precise moment, Captain Munro drove up in a UNIT jeep. He saw Henderson collapsing on the front steps, the Doctor disappearing through the main gates in a wheel-chair, and two very odd looking men clambering into a van driven by a third. The van went off in pursuit of the Doctor.

Immediately Munro swung the jeep round in a tight circle and set off after the van. Driving one-handed he lugged out his service revolver and tried a few shots at the

41

tyres, but with no luck. Tossing the revolver on the seat, he concentrated on his driving.

The Doctor meanwhile was whizzing at tremendous speed down the short, steep hill that led to the hospital. He was very much aware of the pursuing van gaining on him rapidly. It was almost upon him when he spotted a gap in the hedge that bordered the hill. A tiny, narrow track led deep into Oxley Woods. The wheel-chair lurched onto its two side wheels and almost overbalanced as the Doctor flung it into a right-angled turn that sent him rocketing down the path.

The kidnappers' van skidded to a halt at the head of the narrow track. The two huge, silent men jumped out, obviously intending to follow the Doctor on foot.

Then behind them they heard the sound of the UNIT jeep coming after them. As if in obedience to some unspoken command, the men jumped in the van, which accelerated off down the road.

Munro skidded his jeep to a halt at the head of the track. Grabbing his revolver, he shot again at the tyres. Again he missed, and the van disappeared out of sight round the corner of the road. For a moment Munro paused, wondering if he should give chase. He glanced down the little track. A few hundred yards down it he could see the wheel-chair. It lay on its side, one wheel still spinning. In front of the chair there seemed to be a huddled form. Munro decided that recovering the victim was more important than catching the kidnappers, and set off running down the track.

But when he got to the chair he realised that what he had taken for the Doctor's body was no more than a pile of blankets. Munro paused, listening. Faintly he could hear movement going away from him deeper into the woods.

'Hey, come back,' he called. 'It's all right, you're safe now.'

The Doctor was running at full speed through the tangled woods, ignoring the branches that lashed at his face and body. Totally confused by the sudden flurry of events, there was only one thought in his mind. Like a hunted animal making instinctively for its lair, he wanted desperately to reach the safety of the TARDIS.

In one hand he clutched the reassuring shape of the little key that he'd hidden in his shoe. With the other he scrabbled ineffectively at the plaster over his mouth. He paused for a second to try to get it off. Then behind him he heard shouting and the distant sounds of pursuit. The Doctor decided that running was more important than talking and resumed his flight. He had no way of telling that his pursuer was Munro, who wanted only to help him.

On the other side of the woods, Corporal Forbes and his patrol were running too. Forbes had heard the distant sounds of shooting from the hospital and had instinctively led his men in the direction of the trouble. In different parts of the woods, other patrols were converging on the Doctor.

The young sentry left guarding the TARDIS could hear the noises too. He'd been on duty in this gloomy, sinister forest since early dawn. He was cold, tired, hungry and ready to panic. The crack of the shots from Munro's revolver had already alarmed him. Now from all round seemed to come shouts and the sound of men crashing through the woods. He spun round nervously from side to side, trying to cover every direction at once.

Suddenly he caught a glimpse through the trees of a ghostly white figure bearing down upon him. He brought his rifle to his shoulder.

'Halt,' he called in a cracked voice. 'Halt or I fire!'

Hemmed in by the sound of the UNIT patrols moving in all round him, the Doctor suddenly caught a glimpse of the square blue shape of the TARDIS through the trees. Summoning up the last of his strength, the Doctor flung himself towards it in a last desperate sprint. As he burst from the bushes surrounding the clearing, he saw to his horror the soldier with his rifle aimed straight at him. The Doctor tried to shout but the tape was still over his mouth. There was the crack of the rifle shot, a searing pain in his head and then blackness. The Doctor spun round and crumpled to the ground.

Seconds later Forbes and his patrol reached the clearing.

'I had to shoot, Corp,' babbled the sentry. 'He attacked me. Came straight at me!' Forbes looked at the still figure of the Doctor.

'Attacked you, did he? An unarmed man, in a hospital nightshirt?'

'I challenged him, Corporal, honestly. He didn't answer.'

Forbes knelt and examined the Doctor, turning him gently over onto his back. 'He couldn't answer. Somebody's taped his mouth up.' He looked at the Doctor's white face. A smear of blood was startlingly red on the forehead. Forbes felt for a pulse in the neck. He could feel nothing.

Munro ran up to the clearing, saw the group of soldiers gathered round the motionless Doctor.

'What's happened, Corporal? Is the man all right?'

Forbes looked up. 'No sir. I think he's dead.'

5

The Hunting Auton

Captain Munro paced nervously up and down in the hospital entrance hall, rehearsing what he would say in his coming interview with the Brigadier. He sighed. However you put it, it sounded just as bad. He heard the sound of a car drawing up outside and went out onto the hospital steps.

The Brigadier got out of his staff car, cold anger in every line of his stiff figure. Munro threw up a brisk salute. The Brigadier touched his cap brim with his swagger stick in a brief acknowledgement and said, 'Well?'

Munro sighed. It was going to be even worse than he had feared. 'There was some kind of a raid, sir. They knocked out Doctor Henderson and our sentry, and tried to get the patient away.'

'Who did?'

'We're not sure, sir,' said Munro.

'Tried and succeeded, it seems,' said the Brigadier sourly.

'Well, not entirely, sir. I turned up just as they were getting him out of the building. The patient got away in the confusion, they chased him, and I chased them.'

'And lost them.'

'Well – yes sir. You see, the man ran into the woods. He seemed to be making for the police box where we found him. I thought it was more important to get him back.'

'Instead of which the poor chap was shot down by one of our sentries?'

'It was a very confused situation, sir,' said Munro defensively.

'It was a complete and utter botch-up!' snapped the Brigadier. 'How's the poor chap now?'

'Well, that's just it, sir. No one seems to know.'

The Brigadier said, 'I'd better see him.'

'There is one piece of good news, sir,' said Munro hopefully, as they walked along the corridor. 'Our chaps have turned up one of these meteorite things. Or, rather, the bits of one. It's on its way here now.'

'I'm delighted to hear that the Army managed to achieve something, besides the shooting of a harmless civilian,' said the Brigadier as they entered the hospital room.

Doctor Henderson, still a little shaky himself, was leaning over his patient, once more stretched out on the hospital bed. The Doctor lay completely motionless. Henderson and the nurse were applying some instrument to his head.

Henderson looked up and nodded as the Brigadier entered, and said: 'Extraordinary. Quite extraordinary. Look at these readings.'

The Brigadier looked and was none the wiser. He said: 'How is he?'

'This registers the activity of the brain,' explained Henderson. 'Normally this line fluctuates considerably even when a person is unconscious.'

The Brigadier looked at the chart. 'Not a lot going on, eh?' he said, feeling that some comment was expected.

Henderson was impatient. 'There's nothing whatever going on, as you put it.'

'But he isn't dead?'

'No. But you might say he was just barely ticking over.'

'Something to do with that bullet wound,' suggested Munro.

Henderson shook his head. 'That only left a slight graze across the scalp. Couldn't account for this condition.'

The Brigadier was becoming impatient with all this medical mumbo-jumbo. 'Then what does?' he asked.

Henderson rubbed his chin thoughtfully. 'It's only a guess, but I reckon this coma is self-induced.'

'You mean the chap's put himself out?' asked the Brigadier. 'Why would he do that?'

'Again, I'm only guessing,' said Henderson. 'But it could be part of some kind of healing process. A chance for his body to recover from all the stresses it's been suffering.'

The Brigadier moved closer to the bed and studied the sleeping form. Everything about him sounds like the Doctor, he thought. The police box, the strange physical make-up. And he knew me. He really did know me. He knew about the Cyberman and the Yeti. But there's no resemblance. No resemblance at all. The face, the height, the build, the colour of the hair – all utterly and completely different. And yet… The Brigadier could remember so many incredible things about the man he had known as the Doctor. Was a change of appearance any more unbelievable than all the rest?

He turned away from his bed. 'You'll keep me informed of his condition. I'd like to know as soon as he can talk.'

'Yes, of course,' said Henderson. 'Oh, by the way, we found this clutched in his hand.'

Henderson handed the Brigadier a little key. 'We had to prise his fingers open. He was really hanging on to it.'

'Yes,' said the Brigadier thoughtfully, 'he would do.

Thank you, Doctor Henderson.' Followed by Munro, he turned and left the room.

Outside the hospital, a couple of soldiers were standing guard beside a wooden ammunition box.

'That'll be the meteorite fragments, sir,' said Munro. The Brigadier peered inside the box, as a soldier held open the lid. The box was about half-full of chunks of some dull green substance, rather like heat-fused glass.

'All we could find, sir,' said Munro. 'It must have broken up when it hit the ground.'

The Brigadier sniffed. 'Doesn't seem much result for all this effort. Keep searching. See if you can find me a whole one. Oh, and put the box in the boot of my car. Miss Shaw can take a look at it.'

The soldier took the box away and the Brigadier turned back to Munro. 'The police box is already on its way to H.Q. I want a guard on the hospital at all times.'

'Yes, sir,' said Munro. 'We won't lose him again, I promise you.'

The Brigadier looked back at the hospital. 'What puzzles me is, why did those people want to kidnap him?'

'Maybe he was one of them,' suggested Munro. 'They could have been trying to rescue him.'

'Anyone get a good look at them?'

'Better than that, sir,' said Munro proudly. 'We've got a picture of their leader. He produced a glossy photograph and handed it to the Brigadier.

The Brigadier studied the picture, obviously one of those taken on his first visit to the hospital. The photograph showed the Brigadier talking to the crowd of journalists.

'That's him, there, sir,' said Munro. Over the Brigadier's shoulder in the picture there could be seen a man standing, watching. A well-dressed man with handsome, regular features and staring eyes.

'Several people recognised him, sir,' said Munro. 'He was here posing as a pressman.'

'What about the other two?'

'Couldn't really get much of a description,' admitted Munro, 'only that they were very big. And there was something strange, blank-looking about their faces. Probably wearing stocking masks.'

The Brigadier opened the door of his car. 'Three things, Munro. Keep searching for the meteorites; guard that man in the hospital; and keep investigating the kidnap attempt. Call me at H.Q., the minute there's news.' The Brigadier closed the car door and the driver accelerated away. Munro gazed after the departing car. Is that all, Brigadier, he thought to himself. And what do I do in my spare time?

As Harry Ransome drove down the familiar road towards the plastics factory, his mind was in a turmoil. His thoughts kept circling round the letter, the incredible, unbelievable letter that had been waiting for him on his return from his business trip to America.

I'm not just going to accept it, he thought. They owe me an explanation, and I'm going to get it. He drove through the gates and parked in his usual slot in the company car-park. Picking up the bulging brief-case from the seat beside him, he got out of the car and stood still for a moment, bracing himself. A smartly-dressed, dapper little man in his early thirties, he usually radiated the warmth and charm of the top-class salesman. But Ransome's face was grim and determined as he strode into the factory.

The girl behind the reception desk was new to him.

She had a strange, expressionless, doll-like prettiness. She looked up incuriously as he entered.

'My name's Ransome. We haven't met, but I expect you've heard of me. I work here – or I used to. Head of Sales and Design. Been with the firm for years.'

Still she didn't speak. Ransome took a deep breath. 'Just popping in to see Mr Hibbert. Don't worry, he won't mind. We're old friends. It's all right, I know the way.'

Ransome strode determinedly past her and through the door to the factory floor. Then he stopped in amazement. Everything was different. The jolly white-coated girls who worked on the production lines, the old-fashioned machinery turning out dolls' heads and limbs and bodies – it was all gone. The place was completely deserted. Ultra-modern equipment had been moved in, equipment that hummed and whined, carrying out its tasks alone and unaided.

Automation, thought Ransome. Everything's been automated. He walked between the new machines and crossed to a doorway. The door was locked. A notice read 'Restricted Zone – Strictly Private'. Ransome was indignant. They can't do that, he thought. That's my workshop. Used to be my workshop. He glanced round, suddenly overcome by a strange feeling of unease. Then he crossed the factory floor and climbed the flight of steps that led to Hibbert's office.

The moment he was out of sight, the door he had been trying opened. A man stood there, looking towards the flight of stairs. An immaculately-dressed man with handsome, regular features and eyes that seemed to glow.

Ransome gave a perfunctory tap on Hibbert's office door and threw it open. He stood for a moment, looking at the man behind the desk. Good old George Hibbert, he thought ironically. Hasn't changed a bit – on the outside.

Hibbert rose slowly. 'Harry,' he said, in a flat level voice. 'I wasn't expecting you.'

'Weren't you? Then you should have been.' Ransome snatched an envelope from his breast pocket and threw it on Hibbert's desk. 'What's all this about, George?'

Still in the same expressionless voice, Hibbert said, 'The letter explains everything.'

'It explains nothing.' Ransome opened his brief-case, fished out a large doll and dumped it on the desk. Hibbert looked at it incuriously. It was an elaborately-dressed girl doll, with golden curls and a simpering smile. Ransome fished a remote-control unit from the case and pressed a button.

Immediately, the doll struggled to its feet and began to walk slowly across the big leather-topped desk, scattering Hibbert's papers. Ransome pressed a second control and the doll began to talk in a high sweet voice. It said, 'Momma, momma, take me for a walk. Momma, momma, buy me some sweeties. Momma, momma…'

Ransome flung the control onto the desk and the doll became silent. Slowly it toppled onto its face. Ransome drew a deep breath. 'Our famous A.1 Walkie Talkie doll,' he said. 'You do recognise it?' Hibbert said nothing.

Ransome went on: 'When I invented this doll, you promised me full backing. You sent me to the States to try and interest the Americans in joint production. You said if it all worked out, we'd turn the whole factory over to making Walkie Talkies. You were going to make me a partner.'

He paused for breath. Still Hibbert sat motionless and silent. Ransome took wads of papers from the brief-case and slapped them on the desk. 'Well, it's all here. Agreements ready to sign. Advance orders, the lot. And when I get back home, what do I find? A letter cancelling the whole deal and giving me the push!'

Ransome looked appealingly at Hibbert. But still the older man made no response.

Ransome's tone altered. 'George, we worked on this project together. I thought we were friends. You helped me with the plans, you encouraged me. Now you just put the chop on it. Don't you think you owe me some kind of an explanation?'

At last Hibbert looked up. 'There was a cheque enclosed with the letter. The financial compensation was adequate.'

Ransome was ironic. 'Oh yes. All very generous. Only that doesn't happen to be the point. I want to know *why*.'

'There were reasons for the decision,' said Hibbert tonelessly. 'Excellent reasons. I cannot explain further.'

'Why not? Why can't you explain?'

'It's the new policy. We've got a new policy. We are no longer manufacturing dolls. We have turned over to other work.'

'This doll's the best thing we ever came up with,' Ransome insisted. 'You said yourself there was a fortune in it.'

Hibbert repeated, 'We've got a new policy.'

'What about my workshop?' Ransome insisted. 'Why can't I get in there?'

For the first time Hibbert's face showed some animation. In an alarmed voice he said, 'Stay away from there, Harry. You mustn't go in there. It isn't safe.'

'What about my tools, my equipment?'

'We'll send them to you. You must promise not to go

near there. You shouldn't have come back here, Harry. It isn't safe.'

Ransome looked curiously at his old colleague. Hibbert's manner had changed completely. The inhuman coldness had gone. Now there were traces of Hibbert's old self. But he seemed frightened, confused.

'Listen, George,' said Ransome gently. 'I'm sorry I blew up at you. Is anything wrong? Are you in some kind of trouble?'

Hibbert shook his head as if to clear it. He said wildly, 'Harry… Harry, you've got to get away… they'll kill—'

Hibbert stopped talking as the office door was flung open. A man stood in the doorway. An immaculately-dressed man with handsome, regular features and glaring eyes.

Ransome said: 'Who the blazes are you?'

The man said nothing but it was Hibbert who answered in the same cold flat voice in which he had first spoken.

'This is Mr Channing, my new partner. There's no point in going on with this conversation. The letter explained everything. Good day to you.'

Ransome opened his mouth as if to argue but something about the burning glare in Channing's eyes seemed to destroy his will. He packed the doll and the papers back into the brief-case and almost ran from the office, edging past the motionless figure of Channing in the doorway. He could feel those burning eyes following all the way across the factory floor. Not until he was back in his car, driving fast away from the factory, did he begin to feel safe.

As the sound of his car died away, Channing turned coldly to Hibbert. 'You did not handle the situation well.'

Hibbert said: 'It wasn't easy. He'd worked here for many

years. We were – friends.' His voice tailed off. Somehow he knew that friendship was not a word that would have any meaning for Channing.

Channing's cold voice held a hint of puzzlement. 'The letter was clear. The money offered was sufficient. Why did he not accept the situation?'

Hibbert tried again. 'He liked working for me, you see. He was interested in the project, not just the money.'

'The correct letter would have fashioned his response.'

Hibbert rubbed his forehead. He sounded almost angry. 'It isn't as easy as you make it sound. You don't understand people. They're not always so predictable.'

Channing swung round on him. Hibbert backed away in terror as those staring eyes seemed to burn into his brain. But Channing spoke quietly, almost kindly.

'The visit of the man Ransome has disturbed you. But he is gone now. He will not return. All you need do is continue to run the factory as though nothing had changed. That is your sole concern, Hibbert. Do you understand?'

As always when Channing spoke to him in that tone, Hibbert felt calmed and reassured. A sense of clear-headedness and well-being came over him. It was all so simple. All he had to do was follow Channing's orders and everything would be all right. He had to do what Channing told him because… because… Hibbert found that he couldn't remember the reason. But he was quite sure that Channing must be obeyed, that there would be the most terrible consequences if Channing became angry with him. Hibbert's face twitched at the memory of some horror buried deep in his mind. Then he became relaxed again, as he heard Channing's soothing voice.

'Do you understand, Hibbert? Do you understand?'

Hibbert said calmly: 'Yes, I understand.'

Channing turned away and stared broodingly out of the office window at the line of trees which marked the beginning of Oxley Woods.

'Two of the energy units are still missing. The Autons have not succeeded in finding them.'

Hibbert said worriedly: 'Perhaps they broke up on landing.'

'Perhaps. Or they may have buried themselves too deep in the soil of your planet.'

'Do you think that man in the hospital found one? Will you try to capture him again?'

'No. It is too dangerous.'

'If the energy units are buried, how will you find them?'

'They will increase the strength of their pulsation signals. The Auton is searching now. It will find them.'

Hibbert looked at him curiously. 'You talk of these energy units as if they were alive.'

Channing turned and looked at this pitifully inadequate human creature. How limited was its intelligence. How easily its mind could be controlled. Soon these ridiculous little animals would be swept away, replaced as masters of this rich planet by the all-conquering mind of the Nestenes. Still, for the moment it was useful. It must be reassured, humoured.

Channing said gently: 'Energy is a form of life, Hibbert.'

Hibbert's worries persisted. 'What about UNIT? Do you think they suspect the truth?'

Channing smiled coldly. 'Even if they do, their minds will be too limited to accept it – until it is too late. I do not think we have anything to fear from UNIT.'

Sam Seeley came out of the back door of his cottage. With a hasty look to make sure his wife wasn't watching, he scuttled down to his shed, a tumbledown building at the end of the long, overgrown cottage garden. He slipped inside and closed the door behind him. Then, furtively he dragged an old tin trunk from under his workbench and opened the lid. Like a child with a new toy, Sam just couldn't resist taking another look at his treasure. The wonderful find that was going to bring him fame and fortune – once those idiots of soldiers realised that it took a man like Sam Seeley to find things in the woods.

Seeley unwrapped the green globe with trembling fingers, till it lay exposed on the crumpled sheet of tin foil. He stroked it gently.

'Worth a pound or two, you are, me beauty. I'll just hang on to you till they all get a bit keener.'

Sam let his imagination wander, dreaming of a huge cash reward from a grateful government. He'd have his picture in the local paper. Maybe they'd even want him to go on telly. Sam was so wrapped up in his dream of wealth and glory that he scarcely noticed when the globe began to pulse with a greenish glow, gently at first, then with increasing strength.

Not far away in the woods the Auton had been standing motionless under a tree. It was shaped like a man but it was not human. It wore dark, serviceable overalls. Its face was a rough copy of a human face, but blank, unfinished, the features horribly lumpy and crude. It stood, silent, motionless, waiting.

At precisely the moment that the globe in Seeley's trunk began to pulse, the Auton came to life. Its whole body swung round like a radar antenna, first one way and then the other. It swung back towards a particular point and then froze. Then, after a moment it began to move forward in a clumsy, shambling run. It ran in a perfectly straight line, snapping off the branches and bushes that were in its path. Only for big obstacles, like trees, would it turn aside. But it always returned unerringly to its course, pounding towards the signal that was summoning it.

Sam Seeley was wakened from his dreams of glory by a familiar voice. 'Sam, Sam Seeley! What you up to down there?' He peered through the shed window and saw his wife, Meg, hurrying down the path. Instantly Sam tried to put the globe back in the trunk but it slipped from his fingers and rolled under the workbench, still pulsing. Sam threw some old sacking over it.

In the woods the approaching Auton quickened its pace as if the signal were stronger.

Sam looked up innocently as the shed door flew open. His wife, Meg, a thin, depressed looking woman in an old flowered apron, stood looking suspiciously at him.

'What you up to in there, Sam Seeley?'

Sam's face was a picture of virtuous indignation. 'Up to? Nothing. Just a bit of sorting out.'

Meg looked suspiciously round the cluttered shed, and noticed the old tin trunk. 'What you doing with that old box?'

'Nothing.'

Meg had been married to Sam for over twenty years, and by now she disbelieved everything he told her on principle.

'You haven't been thieving again, have you? 'Cause if you have...'

'Oh, that's nice, isn't it?' said Sam. 'Accusing your own husband.'

Meg opened the lid of the trunk and peered inside. It was empty.

'Satisfied?' asked Sam. 'Then how about getting me some grub? I'm hungry.'

'Just you watch your tongue,' said Meg indignantly. 'And don't you go bringing any of your old rubbish in my house.' Slamming the shed door behind her, she disappeared up the garden path and went inside the cottage kitchen.

Sam chuckled to himself. He fished out the glowing globe from beneath the pile of sacking, re-wrapped it in the kitchen foil, put it back into the trunk, then closed the lid. He slid the trunk back under the workbench, then left the shed.

In the woods the Auton stopped its remorseless progress. It swung its huge body in an arc, first one way and then the other, searching for the lost signal. Finding nothing, it simply stood there, waiting for the summons to come again. It could feel no impatience, no tiredness, no hunger. These were human qualities, and the Auton wasn't human. It would wait there for ever if need be, until its orders were changed, or the summoning signal came again.

The Doctor lay stiff and straight, eyes closed, in the hospital bed. He looked rather like the model of a crusader on an old tombstone.

Henderson looked down on him. 'Well, he's out of that deep coma. Seems to be sleeping normally now.'

The nurse said: 'Do you think he's well enough to be handed over to the UNIT people yet?' She spoke a little regretfully, as if she'd grown rather attached to this unusual patient.

'Oh, I think so,' said Doctor Henderson. 'But Mr Beavis is coming down specially to examine him. Saw my report and insisted on having a look.'

The nurse gave him a sympathetic smile. Mr Beavis was the hospital's senior Surgical Consultant. He appeared only rarely, spending most of his time in his Harley Street consulting rooms. His eccentric appearance and high-handed, lordly manner never failed to strike terror into the junior staff.

'But Mr Beavis is a surgeon,' said the nurse, puzzled. 'I don't see—'

'Exactly,' said Henderson cheerfully. 'I gather he thinks this chap is some kind of interesting freak. Probably plans to open him up and sort out his innards for him.'

The nurse shuddered, and Henderson grinned at her. 'Come on, let's leave the poor chap to rest while he can.'

Henderson and the nurse both left the room. As soon as the door closed behind them, the Doctor's eyes opened and he sat bolt upright.

'Interesting freak,' he muttered indignantly. 'Well, nobody's going to sort out *my* innards.' He swung his feet out of the bed, stood up and stretched.

'Now then, I wonder where they put my clothes.' The Doctor looked round the room. His clothes were nowhere to be seen. Cautiously he opened the door a crack, peered out, and then slipped out into the deserted hospital corridor. First he'd find himself some clothes. Then he'd go and find the TARDIS.

6

The Doctor Disappears

At that very moment two sweating soldiers were wrestling the TARDIS into a corner of the UNIT laboratory, while Liz and the Brigadier looked on.

'Right, that'll do,' said the Brigadier, and the soldiers thankfully stopped shoving and left the room.

'All you need now is a key,' said Liz. 'Maybe the police will lend you one.'

'As a matter of fact, Miss Shaw, I already have the key.' The Brigadier produced the little key that Henderson had taken from the Doctor's hand.

The wall 'phone-buzzer sounded and the Brigadier picked up the receiver. He listened for a moment, said: 'Yes, yes, very well,' and put the 'phone down, frowning. He turned to Liz.

'General Scobie is on his way up.'

Liz raised her eyebrows inquiringly.

'He's our Liaison Officer with the Regular Army,' explained the Brigadier. 'Technically, he's my immediate superior. Very important to keep on good terms with *him*. His men are carrying out the search.'

Liz returned to her workbench. 'As long as you don't expect me to salute him.'

The Brigadier heaved an exasperated sigh. 'Really, Miss Shaw, if you could try to be a little less difficult.'

Liz was still in a bad mood because her experiments were going badly. 'I didn't ask to come here, remember?' she said.

The Brigadier's equally acid reply was cut off by the entrance of General Scobie. Scobie was in his middle fifties, with a grizzled grey moustache. He was a rather shy man who took refuge behind a rough military manner, snapping out orders and questions in a gruff voice. But his bark was very much worse than his bite. He and the Brigadier got on extremely well.

Scobie looked round the laboratory, and at the busily-working Liz.

'Sorry to interrupt, Brigadier,' he barked. 'Just thought I'd look in, you know.'

'Always a pleasure to see you, sir,' said the Brigadier smoothly. 'Miss Shaw, may I present General Scobie? Miss Shaw is our new Scientific Adviser.'

Scobie said gruffly: 'You're a lucky feller, Lethbridge-Stewart – having a pretty girl around the place.'

Liz, who was in no mood for frivolity, gave him a quelling look and went on with her work.

The Brigadier hastened to smooth over the moment's awkwardness. 'Miss Shaw is working on the meteorite operation for us,' he said.

Scobie seized the topic thankfully. 'Ah yes, yes. Anything new on that? Papers seem to be going wild. Martians... space-ships... silly season, y'know.' Suddenly Scobie caught sight of the battered old blue police box standing in the corner. His eyes widened. 'What the devil are you doing with a police box?'

Liz looked up. 'As a matter of fact, General Scobie, it isn't a police box at all. It's a camouflaged space-ship.'

Scobie stared at her, then started to laugh. 'Camouflaged space-ship, hey?' he said. 'I like that. Very good, young lady, very good.' He turned to the Brigadier. 'Like to see a sense of humour among the troops. Good for morale, you know, good for morale.'

With some difficulty the Brigadier managed a tight smile.

'Quite sir. Well, I think we should let Miss Shaw get on with her work. Perhaps a drink in my office, sir?' The Brigadier quickly ushered General Scobie out of the laboratory, shooting an exasperated look at Liz over the General's shoulder. Liz chuckled, and went back to her work, feeling rather cheered up by the encounter.

The Doctor strolled along the hospital corridor in his dressing-gown, occasionally exchanging a cheerful nod with a nurse or a fellow patient. Sooner or later, he realised, someone was going to ask him what he was up to. That is if he didn't run slap into Henderson, or his own particular nurse. Suddenly, he heard the familiar sound of Henderson's voice. 'Hope you had a good journey, sir?'

The voice was just round the next corner. Immediately, the Doctor opened the nearest door, looking for a hiding-place. He found himself in a small room, one side of which was lined with lockers. Another door, at the far end, led into a washroom. Footsteps stopped outside in the corridor. Henderson's voice said: 'How were the roads, sir?' Another voice, high-pitched and querulous, answered: 'Shockingly overcrowded, as usual. No room for a decent car these days.' The door to the corridor started to open.

The Doctor dashed through into the washroom. He looked round wildly at the row of washbasins. Then he spotted the shower-stall in the corner… Hastily he began pulling off his dressing-gown.

In the locker-room, Henderson was helping Mr Beavis off with his driving clothes. One of the old boy's many eccentricities was to drive a vintage Edwardian Rolls. He dressed accordingly.

Henderson slipped the long driving cape from Beavis's shoulders and hung it up. Beavis pulled off his Sherlock Holmes deerstalker. The two men walked into the washroom. Beavis took his jacket off and began to wash his hands.

'What are all those toy soldiers doing round the place?'

Henderson had to raise his voice to answer. Loud splashing and tuneless singing was coming from the shower-stall.

'Searching for lost Government equipment. That's how they found the patient, you know, sir.'

Beavis cackled: 'And then they shot him, eh?'

'It was all a bit unfortunate,' agreed Henderson.

A new thought struck Beavis. 'Listen, I've left me car outside. They won't go muckin' about with it, will they?'

Henderson passed the old man a towel and stood by to help him on with his jacket. 'I'm sure it'll be quite safe, sir. As a matter of fact, I've asked them to look after it for you.'

'I thought perhaps a cup of tea in my office, sir?' said Henderson. 'You could take a look at my notes and records. Then we could go and see the patient.'

Beavis settled his jacket onto his shoulders and turned to go. A note of enthusiasm came into his voice. 'What I thought we could do, d'you see… just a brief exploratory operation. Open him up, take a poke around, see what's what.'

The old man's voice faded as Henderson ushered him through to the locker-room and out into the corridor. The door closed behind them. The Doctor's indignant face popped out between the shower curtains. 'Poke around!' he said. 'Poke around! Oh no you don't!'

Wrapped in a towel, the Doctor stepped out of the shower and went through into the locker-room. The lockers contained all kinds of different garments, stored for the hospital's in-patients. The Doctor rooted around and found the locker with his own clothes. He fished them out, and looked at them sadly. The coat was wrinkled, the trousers were baggy, and both were far too small. He shook his head. 'You'd think if they changed the body, they'd remember to change the clothes to fit.' Well, he wouldn't get far looking like a scarecrow. He needed a disguise. Ruthlessly the Doctor began to rummage through all the other lockers, hauling garments out and tossing them on the floor with wild abandon.

Ten minutes later he stood looking at himself in a mirror. The dark trousers were quite a decent fit, and so was the velvet jacket. The frilly white shirt, once the property of an aspiring pop star, added a touch of gaiety. So did the floppy bow tie. The Doctor gave his new appearance an approving nod. In his old body, he'd never bothered about clothes, but in his new appearance they seemed rather important to him.

The Doctor spotted Beavis's cape and deerstalker hanging up. Just what he needed. 'Serve the old butcher right,' he said cheerfully to himself. 'And didn't he say something about a Rolls?' He slipped the cloak round his shoulders and pulled the deerstalker over his eyes. Finally he went through the pockets of his old clothes. 'Sonic screwdriver, TARDIS detector… Yes, it all seems to be there.' Quickly the Doctor transferred his possessions into his new pockets. Then he slipped Beavis's cape round his shoulders, pulled the deerstalker down over his forehead and cautiously opened the door into the corridor.

Hastily he pulled it shut again as once more he heard familiar voices.

'Dammit, Henderson, if those notes are accurate, the feller *must* be a freak,' Beavis was saying.

'They're accurate, I promise you, sir,' Henderson replied. 'But if he is a freak, he seems to be a very healthy one. I don't see that an operation…'

'Where's your sense of adventure?' asked Beavis. 'Haven't had a really interesting operation for years. It'd be a *challenge*.'

The Doctor shuddered to himself as the voices moved away. Then he opened the door again, stepped out into the corridor, and made off hastily in the opposite direction.

As the Doctor strode across the foyer, with a brief nod to the receptionist, a passing medical student said to his friend, 'Old blood-and-bones isn't honouring us for long. He's only just arrived.'

'Good job too,' said the other. 'He's probably finished off poor old Henderson's patient for him already.'

The Doctor emerged onto the steps. A soldier was standing guard on a very handsome vintage Rolls-Royce.

The sentry looked up in alarm as he saw the tall, imposing figure bearing down upon him. They'd impressed it upon him that the old boy was some kind of VIP.

'All present and correct, sir,' said the soldier as the Doctor climbed on board. 'Very handsome vehicle, sir.'

'Harrumph,' replied the Doctor, thanking his lucky

stars that the key was still in the dashboard. The old engine turned over sluggishly, and the Doctor revved it up again.

In the room that had been the Doctor's, Beavis and Henderson were staring, perplexed, at a very empty bed.

'Some kind of prank, is it?' said Beavis querulously.

'He was here just a moment ago,' said Henderson.

A coughing roar was heard from outside. 'My car!' the old man yelped angrily. 'Someone's muckin' about with my car!' He rushed from the room.

With Henderson panting behind, Beavis rushed out onto the main steps, just as the Doctor got the old Rolls engine turning over to his satisfaction.

'Stop, stop,' yelled Beavis. 'Get out of that car at once!' The Doctor raised his hand in a lordly wave, put his foot down hard. He accelerated down the drive, through the main gates, and out of sight.

As the Doctor sped along the road that led through

Oxley Woods he caught sight of the Army patrols, still searching. But it didn't arouse much interest in him. As yet, the Doctor had no idea of the significance of the meteorite shower that had accompanied his arrival on the planet Earth. He had only one idea in his mind – to find the TARDIS, and its key, and resume his travels through Time and Space. He glanced down at the device on the seat beside him. In appearance it was like an old-fashioned pocket-watch. But instead of hands, the dial bore a single needle. That needle always pointed unerringly towards the TARDIS. It was quivering now. With a smile of satisfaction the Doctor sped on his way.

Deep in the woods Corporal Forbes and his patrol were bending excitedly over their detection device. They were on the borders of a small stream which ran through a clearing.

'It's a reading, Corp,' said one of the soldiers excitedly. 'I'm sure it's a reading. Can't seem to see anything, though.'

Forbes squatted on his boot-heels. The reading was strongest at the very edge of the stream. Carefully Forbes began to smooth away the muddy soil, digging gently with his strong fingers. Soon his fingers touched a round smooth shape.

'Shovel,' snapped Forbes, and one of the others hastily passed him a short-handled trench shovel from his pack.

As Forbes dug cautiously, the spherical shape of a meteorite was gradually revealed.

'Must have buried itself in the wet mud, see,' said the Corporal. 'Then the water smoothed over the mud, covered the traces, like. Get Captain Munro on the RT, lad. Tell him the good news.'

As the soldier turned to his field radio, the sphere was already beginning to pulse with a green, unearthly light.

Not far away, an Auton came to life. It spun round in an arc, spun back again, getting a fix on the signals from the sphere. Lurching forward the Auton began its march towards the unsuspecting soldiers.

When Munro arrived in the clearing the sphere, now pulsing strongly and regularly, had been completely dug up. It was resting on sacking in the bottom of an ammunition-box.

Munro looked at the sphere with curiosity. 'Well done, Corporal Forbes, jolly well done. Carry it up to the jeep, will you?'

The two soldiers picked up the ammunition-box by its rope handles. With Munro and Forbes in the lead, the little group headed for the road.

'The Brigadier will want this in the lab at H.Q., right away,' said Munro.

'Going to drive it up yourself, sir?' asked Forbes. Munro considered; the idea was tempting. But other patrols were still searching. He was needed on the spot to co-ordinate their efforts. Anyway, thought Munro, fair's fair. Forbes had done well to find the meteorite. He deserved to be the one to hand it over.

'I think that honour should be yours, Corporal,' said Munro as they reached the jeep. 'I'll let the Brigadier know you're on your way.'

Two soldiers lowered the ammunition-box carefully into the back of the jeep. They lashed the box into place to make it secure. Forbes got into the driving seat.

'Quick as you can, Corporal,' said Munro. 'But no accidents!'

Forbes grinned. He was a very experienced driver. He'd never had an accident in his life. At a nod from Munro, he started the jeep rolling and disappeared down the country lane, with a roar of exhaust.

'Lucky blighter,' said one of the soldiers enviously. 'He'll be down the pub tonight, while we're camping out in the wild, wet woods.'

Briskly, Munro turned to them. 'Let's not rest on our laurels, eh? Quite a number of those things came down. So far we've turned up one broken one and one whole one. Got to do better than that, haven't we?'

With an inward sigh, the soldiers shouldered their detection gear and returned to the search.

Once the sphere was in the jeep, the Auton realised that pursuit was hopeless. The energy unit was moving away too fast. The Auton stopped, apparently baffled. But the tiny fragment of intelligence that animated the Auton was also a part of the supreme brain of the Nestenes. Part of it, and in constant communication with it. That particular Auton became motionless. The problem no longer concerned it. Fresh orders had been transmitted to one of its fellows, better placed for immediate action.

Corporal Forbes was whistling cheerfully as he drove through the woods. Decent of young Munro to let him deliver the meteorite to H.Q. Some officers would have hogged that job themselves. Taken all the credit, too. Might be a spot of leave in this, with any luck. Maybe even another stripe.

These happy thoughts were suddenly interrupted. A figure stepped from the woods ahead of his jeep. Big chap, wearing overalls. He just stood there in the middle of the road, waiting. Hitch-hiker probably, thought Forbes. Some

70

hopes, this trip.

He made a negative wave of his hand and moved the wheel to drive round the obstruction. But the figure dodged suddenly in front of the jeep, and Forbes had to jam on the brakes to avoid hitting it. The jeep skidded to a halt, its nose in the roadside ditch. Forbes jumped out, shaken and furious.

'You stupid great oaf,' he yelled. 'Might have got killed. Why don't you…'

His voice tailed away as, for the first time, he got a clear look at the giant figure bearing remorselessly down on him. The bloke was enormous, he thought. A giant. And the face! Blank and lumpy and shapeless, like a waxwork left in the sun.

Forbes became aware that the giant was ignoring him and making straight for the ammunition-box lashed to the back of the wrecked jeep. From the corner of his eye, he saw that the lid of the box had flown open. The sphere was flashing rapidly with a kind of furious brightness. Forbes ran to the back of the jeep and grabbed his rifle. Training it on the advancing figure, he stood guard over the box.

'Now listen, mate,' said Forbes, his voice showing none of the panic he was beginning to feel. 'This is government business, see, so just you clear off! I don't want to open fire, but just you believe me, if I've got to, I will.'

His words had absolutely no effect on the advancing figure, now coming very close. Forbes, realising that his enemy wasn't even human, opened fire without the slightest hesitation. He emptied a full clip of bullets into the massive chest. The giant was by now so close that Forbes plainly saw the line of holes appear across the breast of the dark coveralls. But there was no blood, thought Forbes frantically.

71

No blood, and the thing just kept on coming.

Swinging his empty rifle as a club, Forbes landed a tremendous blow on the huge, smooth head. The giant staggered, then smashed the rifle from his grasp, casually, as if swatting a fly. The last thing Forbes saw, as another blow struck him to the ground, was that blank, expressionless face looming over him.

The Auton lifted the body of Corporal Forbes in one hand and tossed it into the ditch. Then moving to the back of the jeep, it took hold of the ammunition-box. The tough manilla ropes snapped like cotton. The Auton lifted the box clear of the jeep, and carrying its flashing, pulsating burden almost reverently, disappeared amongst the trees.

In the restricted zone of the plastics factory, strange alien machinery whirred and hummed and glowed. There came a soft glugging sound as the plastic mix flowed through the pipes. In the centre of the area stood a vast opaque container, shaped very like a coffin. Thick pipes coiled around it, feeding in nutrients. Channing stood watching with quiet satisfaction as deep inside the container something moved and stirred, and grew. Along the walls stood a motionless line of Autons. They seemed to be watching the thing in the tank, waiting eagerly for something to happen.

A buzzer sounded from the doorway. Channing did not move. 'Yes?'

A nervous voice said, 'It's me. Hibbert.'

Channing touched a control button and the door slid open. Hibbert entered cautiously. He hated coming to this place. 'General Scobie has arrived.'

Channing nodded. 'I have almost finished.' He turned his burning eyes on Hibbert. 'I shall need more carbon disulphide tomorrow.' The creature in the tank needed constant nourishment if it was to grow and live. Hibbert glanced curiously at the coffin-shaped tank. He hadn't been told what was in there. He didn't like to think about it.

Channing watched him. 'It would be better if you did not come to this section again. We are approaching a critical point. It could be dangerous for you.'

Hibbert looked at the motionless Autons lining the wall.

'I thought you had control over them. You said they were just walking weapons.'

Channing said softly: 'I have *some* control over them. But they also have a life of their own. Their over-riding function is to kill. You will appear to them as just another target.'

Hibbert shuddered, and thankfully followed Channing from the room. The thing in the tank continued to move and grow. The line of Autons watched and waited. At the feet of one of them was an ammunition-box. But now it was empty.

7

The Horror in the Factory

Angrily the Brigadier snapped into the 'phone: 'For heaven's sake, man, what happened?'

Munro's voice was apologetic. 'We just don't know, sir. The jeep was in the ditch. So was Corporal Forbes, with his neck broken. No sign of the ammo-box or the meteorite.'

'Could it have been an accident?'

Munro sounded dubious. 'It could, sir. But Forbes was an expert driver. He *could* have driven into a ditch and broken his neck in the fall. The box with the meteorite *could* have broken loose in the crash. But in that case where is it? We've searched the entire area.'

'Well, keep searching! I'll try to send you down some more men. Let me know as soon as there's news.'

The Brigadier went to see Liz Shaw and told her the bad news. 'It seems as if somebody, or something, doesn't want us to get hold of one of those meteorites,' he concluded gloomily. The internal 'phone on the wall buzzed and he sighed in exasperation as he grabbed the receiver.

'Yes, now what?'

'Main gate security here, sir. Someone insists on seeing you.'

'Didn't you give him the usual cover-story?'

'Yessir. Told him this building was a branch of the Pensions Department, and we'd never heard of you. He said nonsense, it was UNIT H.Q., and he insisted on seeing Brigadier Lethbridge-Stewart. Er, he said you'd pinched some of his property, sir,' finished the voice apologetically.

'What does he look like?'

'Tall thin bloke, sir, old-fashioned clothes. Driving an old-fashioned car, come to that.'

The Brigadier was jubilant. 'Whatever you do, don't let him get away.'

'He doesn't *want* to get away, sir,' said the voice. 'He wants to come in and see you. Most insistent he is.'

'Then don't stand there dithering, man,' said the Brigadier rather unfairly. 'Send him in at once.'

He turned to Liz, almost spluttering with excitement. 'It's him. That chap. He's actually had the cheek to turn up here. How the blazes did he find this place?'

'Wait and ask him,' suggested Liz practically. A few minutes later the Doctor was shown into the room.

He strode across to the astonished Brigadier and shook him warmly by the hand. 'Lethbridge-Stewart, my dear fellow!' He looked at the TARDIS and patted it affectionately. 'And here she is, all safe and sound. How kind of you to look after her!'

From behind her laboratory bench, Liz watched the Doctor with interest. This was a very different figure from the deathly-still form she'd seen stretched out on the hospital bed. It was obvious that the Doctor, if that was who he was, was now fully recovered. He was tall and elegant in the old-fashioned clothes that seemed to suit him so well. And he positively crackled with life and energy, completely overwhelming the somewhat stunned Brigadier.

'Now then, old chap,' the Doctor went on briskly, 'there's just the little matter of the key. Don't happen to have it, do you?'

'As a matter of fact I do,' said the Brigadier. 'But it doesn't seem to work.'

'Ah, but it will for me,' said the Doctor, with a charming smile. 'It's personally coded, you see, keyed to my molecular structure.' And he held out his hand.

But the Brigadier didn't respond. 'Not so fast. I've got one or two questions to ask you.'

'Questions? My dear chap, it's not a bit of use asking me questions. I've lost my memory, you see.'

The Brigadier was sceptical. 'Have you now? That's very convenient.'

'Not so much lost it exactly,' explained the Doctor, 'as had it taken away. Not all of it, of course. I mean I remember you quite clearly. But quite a lot of other things are a bit cloudy. Things will probably come back to me in time.' He smiled, as if everything had been made perfectly clear.

'I see. So you claim to be suffering from some kind of partial amnesia?'

The Doctor looked distressed. 'You do like to spell things out, don't you?'

'And you also claim to be the man I once knew as "the Doctor"?'

'That's it, old chap, you're getting there,' said the Doctor encouragingly. Liz suppressed a smile.

'And yet,' said the Brigadier triumphantly, 'your whole appearance is totally different. How do I know you're not an impostor?'

The Doctor seemed delighted. 'Ah, but you don't, old chap, you don't! Only I know that.' He noticed a mirror and immediately began pulling faces into it. 'How do you like my new face, by the way? I wasn't too sure about it myself at first, but it's beginning to grow on me. And it's flexible, you know, very flexible.' To prove his point, the Doctor began to pull a variety of extraordinary faces.

The Brigadier took a deep breath and sank rather groggily onto a laboratory stool. 'All right, Doctor, all right! Say I accept this rigmarole, there are still quite a few things to be explained.'

Liz, deciding she'd been ignored long enough, cleared her throat meaningfully. The Brigadier waved a distracted hand towards her. 'This is Miss Shaw, our new Scientific Adviser.' The Doctor was waggling his eyebrows into the mirror.

'Did you know that on the planet Delphon they communicate only with their eyebrows?' He waggled his eyebrows ferociously at Liz. 'That's Delphon for how do you do.' He grinned infectiously and Liz couldn't help smiling back. There was something very engaging about this colourful madman. 'How do you do,' she said. 'What are you a Doctor of, by the way?'

He waved his hand airily. 'Practically everything, my dear, practically everything.'

The Brigadier harrumphed. 'You arrived last night slap in the middle of a shower of very unusual meteorites.'

The Doctor said: 'Did I really now? How fascinating.'

Briefly the Brigadier summarised recent events. The meteorite shower, the finding of the Doctor, the attempted kidnapping and the disappearance of the one whole meteorite that had been found. The Doctor listened with an air of deep interest.

'So you see,' said the Brigadier, 'I can't possibly let you leave until I'm sure there's no connection—'

The Doctor interrupted: 'That's most unfair. I've no

recollection of last night. Even that kidnapping business seems just a sort of nightmare...' Suddenly his attention was attracted by the fragments on the lab bench. 'What are these?'

Liz said: 'Those are fragments of something the Brigadier thought was a meteorite.'

The Doctor looked at her. 'And you don't?' He began to finger the fragments, turning them over and over. 'Plastic!' he said in a surprised tone. 'Surely this is some form of plastic?'

Liz nodded. 'Apparently. But it's not thermo-plastic, and neither is it thermo-setting. And there are no polymer chains.'

The Doctor's manner was now completely serious. Liz watched in fascination as his long fingers turned the fragments over and over on their tray. He weighed some pieces in his hand. 'Most interesting. I wonder what was inside.'

'Inside?'

'Well, it's obvious, isn't it, this was some kind of hollow sphere?' Deftly his fingers assembled the pieces into a curved shape.

'I'd say the space in the middle was about three thousand cubic centimetres, wouldn't you agree?'

Liz looked at him with new respect. The calculation, if it was accurate, had been done with astonishing speed.

The Brigadier had been watching the two of them with interest. It looked as if they would make a good team. He stood up. 'Do I gather you're going to help us – Doctor?'

'If I do, will you give me back the key to the TARDIS?'

The Brigadier nodded. 'Certainly – once this matter has been satisfactorily cleared up.'

The Doctor looked keenly at him. There was a hint of resentment in his eyes. Then he smiled, seeming to accept the situation. 'In that case, Brigadier, I suggest you allow Miss Shaw and myself to get on with our work.' The Doctor turned back to Liz. 'Do I have to call you Miss Shaw? Should be Doctor Shaw, I suppose, really. Or even Professor Shaw?'

'Just Liz will do fine.'

'Splendid!'

The Brigadier said, 'Right then, I'll leave you to it.'

'Just a moment, old chap,' said the Doctor. 'How many of these meteorite things came down?'

'About fifty, near as the radar people could estimate.'

The Doctor frowned. 'And all you've found is this?' He indicated the tray of fragments.

'That, and the whole one, which disappeared on the way here.'

The Doctor slipped out of his cape and threw it across a stool. 'Well, it's obvious what's been happening, isn't it? Before your search could get really under way, most of these things were collected.' The Doctor looked from Liz to the Brigadier. 'Collected and taken somewhere. Question is – where?'

Harry Ransome steered his car carefully down the bumpy forest track. One half of his mind knew that what he was planning was completely daft. But he was determined to go on with it.

After his extraordinary interview with George Hibbert, he'd driven very fast to the local market town and treated himself to several drinks. He went over the interview in his mind time and time again... the strange remote manner of

80

old George, almost as though he'd been hypnotised… the way he'd suddenly seemed more like himself as he'd warned of danger… the arrival of Channing with his burning eyes… the way George had suddenly become a zombie again.

The more he thought about it, the more convinced Ransome had become that there was something very wrong indeed at the factory. Perhaps George was being threatened, or blackmailed. Maybe they had him under some kind of drug. After his fourth drink, Ransome was certain that for George's sake, as well as his own, he had to investigate further. He'd thought of telling the police. But what was there to tell them? The grumbles of a discontented ex-employee? No, first he had to find evidence. In this mood, Ransome had left the pub and gone to look for a hardware shop.

The track became too narrow to drive any further. He stopped the car and got out. From the boot he produced a pair of heavy-duty wire-cutters. He moved through the trees to the wire fence that marked the boundary between the factory and the woods.

Inside the factory, General Scobie's tour had come to an end. He'd expressed polite interest in all the impressive new automated machinery. Now the real purpose – the very flattering purpose – of his visit had been reached.

Scobie was a genuinely shy and modest man. It had never occurred to him that anyone would ever consider him as any kind of celebrity. He had been astonished when Hibbert had contacted him, and had needed quite a bit of persuasion before agreeing. 'Just a simple soldier, you know. Doing my duty.' 'Exactly, General,' Hibbert had said, 'that's just the sort of people we want. Not the showy celebrities, always getting in the papers and on television, but the ones who really keep the country going.' Eventually Scobie had agreed to come to the factory.

Now, in the factory's Replica Room, he was feeling a little hurt. The blank-faced dummy he was looking at bore only a very rough resemblance to him. Channing hastened to explain: 'You see, General, this is just the first draft, so to speak. Prepared from measurements and drawings. For the final process we need your actual presence. If you wouldn't mind standing over there?'

Channing indicated a sort of upright coffin, surrounded with complex instruments. Gingerly, Scobie stepped inside. Immediately, the instruments surrounding him sprang to life. They hummed and whirred and clicked and buzzed excitedly.

'Every detail of your appearance is being recorded, General,' explained Channing. 'The measurements of the facial planes are accurate to millionths of a centimetre.'

Scobie grinned uneasily. 'Jolly impressive,' he said as the instruments fell silent, and Channing helped him to step out. 'I hope it all turns out all right.'

'It will, General,' said Channing solemnly. 'I can promise you that.'

Ransome meanwhile was dodging from machine to machine across the factory floor. Not that there was anyone about to see him. The whole place was deserted. He reached the door to the Restricted Area, and set to work, using his wire-cutters and an improvised crowbar. Savagely he wrenched at the lock, and in a few minutes he had it open. He slipped inside.

Once through the door, he looked round him in astonishment. The machinery here was far more advanced in design, more alien in purpose, than anything out on the factory floor. Fascinated, he moved towards the huge coffin-shaped tank that dominated the centre of the area. Lights flashed and machinery hummed, as if in warning as he moved closer, trying to get a clear look at the huge thing that writhed sluggishly inside the tank.

Ransome had failed to notice the line of silent Autons as they stood motionless against the wall behind him. Absorbed in what he was looking at, he didn't see at first when one of them, the nearest, turned its head to look at him, and then suddenly came to life, taking a step forwards. On its second step, some instinct warned Ransome and he looked behind him. He leaped back as the giant figure came towards him.

The thing held out its hand in a curious pointing gesture. Then, to Ransome's unbelieving horror, the giant hand dropped away from the wrist on some kind of hinged joint. The hand dangled limply to reveal a tube, projecting from the wrist. It was like the muzzle of a gun.

For a moment Ransome stood terrified, then he instinctively hurled himself to one side. A sizzling bolt of energy whizzed past his head, drilling a plate-sized hole in the steel wall. Ransome look at it incredulously, and the Auton raised its hand to fire again.

By pure chance, Ransome made the one move that could save his life. He ducked round the side of the plastic coffin, sheltering behind it. The Auton paused. An overriding point in its programming was that the tank and its contents must not be harmed.

Lowering its wrist-gun, the Auton began to stalk Ransome round the tank, waiting for the chance of a clear shot at him. By keeping the tank between them Ransome

was able to edge near the door. He made a sudden dash through it, leaving the shelter of the tank. The Auton fired another energy-bolt, missing Ransome's head by inches, and blasting another hole in the wall. Then it pursued Ransome out onto the factory floor.

Another energy-bolt whizzed past Ransome's head as he dodged between the machinery. There followed a terrifying game of hide-and-seek. Ransome ducked and dodged around the machinery, desperately avoiding the hunting Auton. He realised that the creature must have some kind of intelligence. It consistently managed to block his way to the exit. All time it was edging closer and closer, confining him to one corner of the factory. With a feeling of terror Ransome realised that he was running out of hiding-places. He could see the Auton coming closer, wrist-gun raised.

Suddenly he heard footsteps and voices. He peered cautiously from behind a machine casing. Coming towards him across the factory area was Hibbert, talking to a man in army officer's uniform. Ransome was about to call for help, when he saw Channing following along behind. Ransome kept silent. Something told him that he would get no help from Channing. As he watched, Channing suddenly stopped walking. Those strange, burning eyes swept round the factory floor. Ransome shuddered and ducked out of sight.

As soon as he made contact with the consciousness of the Auton, Channing knew everything that had happened. He knew of Ransome's breaking in, the hunt across the factory, the fierce desire of the Auton to destroy the intruder. Swiftly Channing weighed up the factors. It was too soon to risk Scobie seeing anything that would disturb him. Channing flashed a mental command and the Auton stepped back in a shadowed corner and became motionless.

Instantly, Ransome seized his chance, weaving between the machinery and dashing out through the doorway by which he had entered.

Channing walked up to Scobie and Hibbert, who had been waiting for him in some puzzlement.

'Everything all right?' asked Hibbert.

'Forgive me, gentlemen,' said Channing, 'just a sudden problem, something I must attend to later.'

'Jolly quiet round here,' said Scobie. 'Doesn't seem to be anyone in the place.'

Hibbert said: 'We're turning over to full automation, General. The factory virtually runs itself.'

Scobie chuckled. 'Splendid. Don't get any of this strike nonsense, eh? Didn't I see a big chap in overalls just now, though?'

Channing said: 'We still have one or two men about the place, for the heavy work. Your car's through this way, General Scobie.'

They walked to where the General's limousine stood waiting. Scobie held out his hand. 'Well, goodbye, gentlemen. Been a most interesting afternoon.' Channing hesitated, hands still clasped behind him. It was Hibbert who stepped forward and shook Scobie's hand.

'Goodbye, sir, and thank you once again for coming down here. We know how busy you must be.'

'You'll let me see the model of me when it's really finished?'

'You will certainly see it, General,' said Channing, '… when the time comes.'

Scobie got into his car, and was driven away. Channing and Hibbert looked after him a moment, and then walked back into the factory.

Ransome meanwhile was struggling through the hole he had cut in the wire. He ran for his car, jumped in, and reversed as fast as he could up the forest track. Not until he was back on the road and driving very fast towards London did he even begin to feel safe. Suddenly, he saw a small group of soldiers emerge from the forest. He jammed on his brakes and wound down the car window.

'Hey… hey you!'

The NGO in charge of the patrol came up to the car.

'Anything wrong, sir?'

'There's something terribly wrong. They just tried to murder me!'

The Corporal looked at Ransome's wild-eyed face with

some caution.

'Better tell the police then, sir. There's a police station down in the village.'

'It's not a matter for the police. Look, let me talk to somebody senior. One of your officers.'

The Corporal considered for a moment, then decided to play it safe. Probably the man was just a nut, but you never knew.

'Captain Munro's in the Command Tent. At the end of that lane, just down there. You could have a word with him.'

Ransome's car was already speeding down the road. The Corporal shook his head, and he and his men resumed their patrol.

In the factory's security area, Channing and Hibbert stood looking at a small screen. Hibbert said: 'You're sure it was Ransome? You didn't actually see him.'

Channing indicated the Auton, now once more standing in line with its fellows. 'The Auton saw him. It comes to the same thing.' Channing looked at Hibbert almost with pity. These humans with their limited, separate minds. How could they understand the essential unity of the Nestene consciousness? He touched a control and a bright cobwebby pattern appeared on the screen. 'The detection scanner has registered his brain-print.'

Hibbert looked frightened. 'What will you do?'

'Send the Autons to destroy him.'

'No, Channing, no! You can't just kill him! He was my friend.'

Channing came close, his burning eyes boring into Hibbert's very brain. He spoke soothingly: 'It is necessary,

Hibbert. He saw all this. He saw the Autons. No one can see those things and live. No one except you, Hibbert. Think, and you will see that it is necessary.'

Hibbert's mind became calm. Of course Ransome had to die. It was unfortunate, but logical. 'How will the Autons find him?'

Channing said: 'They are programmed now to detect his brain-print and destroy him on sight.' He looked at the pattern on the screen. 'He is still in the area. Soon they will find him.' As if at a silent command, the line of Autons jerked into life, and marched silently from the room.

Hibbert said: 'You are sending all of them to hunt for Ransome?'

'If they find Ransome they will kill him. But that is not their primary purpose. All of the energy units have been recovered or accounted for. All except one. But that one is the most important of all.' Channing swung round on Hibbert, his eyes burning with a fierce unearthly light. 'Before the invasion can begin, we must find the swarm leader!'

Sam Seeley took a noisy swig from his mug of tea, and looked up defiantly at his wife. 'How do you know it weren't an accident, then, eh? How do you know?'

Meg's voice was hushed with drama. 'The soldiers found one of them things that came down in the woods. Poor lad was driving it back to London, on one of those little jeeps.'

'So he had a crash,' said Sam. 'Nothing in that. Road accidents happening all the time.'

Meg leaned forward. 'His neck were broken, clean through. And his rifle were beside him, the barrel all twisted. They say there was a look of terrible fear on his face.'

Sam shivered. 'Lots of gossip,' he said uneasily. 'Old wives' tales.'

Meg took another sip of tea. 'Maybe so. But I'm glad I never found one of those things.'

'Lucky for anyone who did,' said Sam defiantly. 'You see, they'll be offering a reward soon.'

'Maybe,' said Meg. 'And maybe you wouldn't live long enough to enjoy it.'

She finished her tea and stood up. 'Well, I'm off down the shop.' She gave Sam a peck on the cheek, and put on her coat. Sam was staring into his tea mug, obviously a very worried man. As she came out of the front door, Meg smiled to herself. She knew well enough that her Sam was up to something. He'd been acting funny and mysterious ever since that night in the woods. Well, maybe she'd managed to scare some sense into him. Barney, Sam's old lurcher dog, was dozing in the front garden. He wagged his tail, but couldn't be bothered to get up.

Back in the cottage Sam stood up, undecided. Course, it was just a lot of silly gossip. Still, he couldn't keep that thing in the shed forever. Maybe it was time for a little chat with those soldier boys. Couldn't do any harm to sound them out. He might even drop one or two hints.

In the UNIT Command Tent, Captain Munro looked with concern at the terrified figure on the other side of the trestle table. Ransome's hands were shaking so much that he had to clasp the mug of strong army tea with both hands. His teeth chattered against the rim of the mug as he drank.

Munro said gently: 'I'm sorry, sir, but the story isn't all that clear. You broke into the factory, and someone tried to kill you?'

Ransome made a mighty effort. 'Not *someone*. *Something*. A creature. There were lots of them. They must be making them in the factory. No proper eyes... no hair... a lumpy face... it came after me.' Ransome began to shiver uncontrollably.

'It's all right, you're safe now,' said Munro soothingly. 'Now then, you say it had a gun?'

Ransome spluttered with the effort to explain the horror he had seen. 'Not *had* a gun... the gun was part of it... its hand just fell away, hung there...' He looked at Munro wildly, as if begging him to understand and believe him.

Munro came to a decision. 'Look, sir, all this is a bit above my head. I'd like you to tell this story to my Brigadier. He'll know how to handle things.'

Munro raised his voice. 'Sergeant! I want this man taken to UNIT H.Q., right away.'

Liz Shaw and the Doctor were bent over the tray of meteorite fragments. The Doctor moved the scanning equipment gently across the surface. Liz said, 'Are you getting a reading?'

The Doctor shook his head. 'Nothing.'

'Right, that's it, then,' said Liz in some disgust. 'We've tried every test and, except that we *think* it's some kind of totally unknown plastic, we've got nowhere.'

The Doctor shrugged. 'Well, we did our best. After all, with this primitive equipment they've given us...'

Liz gestured round the laboratory. 'Primitive? Come on now, Doctor, that's not really fair. We've got lasers, spectographs, micron probes.'

The Doctor sniffed disparagingly. 'What we really need is a lateral molecular rectifier. That'd give us the answer in 'no time.'

'And what on earth is a lateral molecular thingummy?'

'Nothing on Earth, unfortunately. But I've got one in the TARDIS.'

'You really do keep your scientific equipment in that old police box?'

The Doctor looked at her solemnly. 'My dear young lady, you simply wouldn't believe what I keep in there.'

'All right, then,' said Liz, 'get the thing out. We've tried everything else.'

The Doctor looked crestfallen. 'The trouble is the – er, box is still locked. And the Brigadier refuses to part with the key.' He looked at Liz hopefully. 'You might be able to persuade him.'

In his office, the Brigadier was listening with mounting incredulity to Harry Ransome's story. Ransome was calmer now, more coherent. He went over the whole story from his first visit to America, to his final escape from the Auton. When he was finished Ransome sat back and took a deep breath. He looked at the Brigadier ruefully. 'Don't believe a word of it, do you? Can't say I blame you.'

Embarrassed, the Brigadier fiddled with a little key on his desk blotter.

'Now, I didn't say that, Mr Ransome. As a matter of fact we, at UNIT, are particularly interested in that part of the world.'

There was a tap on the door and the Brigadier looked up as Liz Shaw entered. 'Excuse me,' she said with a glance at the visitor.

The Brigadier was irritated at the interruption. Time the girl learned some discipline. She was in UNIT now.

'Not now, Miss Shaw.'

'This is rather urgent. You see, the Doctor thinks—'

The Brigadier was outraged. 'Miss Shaw, your work in the laboratory is only a small part of a very complex operation. Mr Ransome has come to me with a very interesting story, and I want to hear it without interruptions.'

Ignoring Liz, the Brigadier rose and pointed to a wall-map. 'Now exactly where is this plastics factory of yours?'

Ransome peered at the map, and then said: 'Just there.'

The Brigadier nodded. 'Exactly. Close to the borders of Oxley Woods. Some very funny things have been happening there.'

The two men had turned their backs on Liz to study the map. She was left standing in the doorway, furious at her abrupt dismissal. Suddenly she saw the little key on the desk. Without a word, she snatched it up and swept from the room, slamming the door behind her with a crash that shook the room.

The Brigadier winced, then resumed his place behind the desk.

'Now then, Mr Ransome, let's just run through the main points of this story of yours again.'

Liz stormed into the laboratory, and thrust the little key into the Doctor's hand. 'Of all the pompous, overbearing idiots,' she said furiously, 'that Brigadier takes the biscuit!'

The Doctor looked at the key in amazement. 'He gave it to you – just like that?'

'Not exactly. I took it.'

'Oh dear,' said the Doctor. 'I'm afraid he's going to be very cross with you.'

Taking the key from her hand, he looked at her with

a worried frown. He glanced from the tray of meteorite fragments to the TARDIS and then back at Liz. He seemed torn by indecision.

'Hadn't you better get on with it?' said Liz.

The Doctor sighed. 'Yes, I'm afraid I had. Thank you, my dear. Goodbye.'

The Doctor crossed to the TARDIS and slipped the key in the lock. The door opened and the Doctor stepped inside, closing the door behind him.

Liz looked at the closed door in amazement, waiting for the Doctor to emerge. Why had he said goodbye like that? Suddenly she heard a strange groaning and wheezing coming from the TARDIS. It was like the sound of some powerful but rather ancient engine creaking into life.

That sound reached the Brigadier in his office. He looked down at his desk, registered the absence of the key. To Ransome's astonishment he gave a bellow of rage and ran from the room.

The groaning and roaring was still going on as the Brigadier dashed into the laboratory. The TARDIS was shuddering and vibrating now. Liz had backed away from it and was watching in astonishment.

'The key,' spluttered the Brigadier, raising his voice above the din. 'You gave it to the Doctor?'

Liz nodded. 'He said he kept some vital equipment in there.'

'Equipment?' roared the Brigadier. 'You little idiot! He's escaped! We shan't see him again.'

The roar of the TARDIS rose to a shattering crescendo. 'There you are,' shouted the Brigadier. 'He's going!'

Suddenly there was a loud bang from inside the

TARDIS. The groaning noise subsided, the TARDIS door flew open, and a cloud of smoke billowed out. In the middle of the smoke appeared the Doctor, coughing and choking. He waved his handkerchief to clear the smoke and then spotted the Brigadier and Liz. He gave them a rather sheepish smile, and closed the TARDIS door.

'I was just testing, you know. Just testing.'

'Doctor, you tricked me,' said Liz accusingly.

The Doctor sighed. 'I'm afraid I did, my dear. Please forgive me. The temptation was very strong. You see, I suddenly couldn't bear the thought of being tied to one time-zone and one planet.' He turned to the Brigadier. 'Sorry, old chap. I won't do it again.'

'You certainly won't,' said the Brigadier grimly. 'Give me that key, Doctor.'

'Must I?' said the Doctor plaintively. 'As you saw, the TARDIS isn't working any more.'

He looked so unhappy that the Brigadier couldn't help feeling sorry for him. He cleared his throat and said gruffly: 'Well – if you give me your word not to try and escape again.'

The Doctor sank despondently onto a stool. 'I couldn't escape now if I wanted to – not in the TARDIS. They've changed my dematerialisation code.'

'Who's changed what?'

'The Time Lords. Oh, the despicable, underhanded lot!' said the Doctor indignantly.

'You can talk,' said Liz. She hadn't entirely forgiven the Doctor his trickery.

Hastily, the Doctor turned to the Brigadier. 'Well now, about this little problem of yours. Miss Shaw and I have come to a dead end, I'm afraid.'

'It's because we haven't got a lateral molecular rectifier, you see,' said Liz, with a look at the Doctor.

'A what?' said the Brigadier. 'I told you I can get you any equipment you need.'

'Just a little joke,' said the Doctor hastily. 'The thing is, we need something more to work on.'

'I think I may be able to provide it for you,' said the Brigadier. 'Will you both come to my office, please? There's someone I'd like you to talk to. We're all going to take a little trip down to Essex, to visit a plastics factory.'

8

The Auton Attacks

Sam Seeley shuffled his feet uneasily, twisting his old cloth cap between his fingers. His gaze wandered all round the tent, trying to avoid the sceptical eyes of the young officer behind the table.

Munro said sharply: 'Come on now, Mr Seeley, you're wasting my time. Have you got something to tell me, or haven't you?'

'I'm only trying to help, like,' said Sam vaguely. 'You see, I knows these woods, like, knows every rabbit-hole.'

'Poacher, are you?'

'Let's just say I'm self-employed.'

'I'm still trying to work out why you came to see me.'

Sam groaned inwardly. This conversation wasn't going at all the way he'd imagined it. No one seemed at all interested in his subtle hints. All he was getting was a lot of uncomfortably direct questions.

He tried again. 'See, if I knew a bit about what you was looking for...' Munro's voice was stern. 'I'm afraid I can't tell you that, Mr Seeley. But I can tell you this. The objects we're searching for are extremely dangerous. One man has been killed already.'

Sam made a final try. 'I reckon it'd be worth a fair bit of money – if anyone did happen to know where he could put his hand on one?'

Munro leaned forward. 'It'd be worth quite a long spell in prison for someone withholding information, if someone did know where to find one, and didn't inform us. Of course, if that someone came forward like a public-spirited citizen – well, there might possibly be some question of a small reward. Some kind of finder's fee.'

Sam brightened immediately. Even a small reward was better than nothing. He pulled up one of the wooden chairs and sat down, leaning forward confidentially. 'Well, it were like this, you see... I were checking me traps last night in Oxley Woods when all of a sudden...'

When Sam's wife returned from her shopping the little cottage was silent and empty. She wasn't particularly surprised. Her Sam was in the habit of appearing and disappearing as the fancy took him. She went out of the back door and called: 'Sam, Sam, you out there!' There was no answer. On impulse she went down the garden and opened the shed door. No Sam. She was about to shut the door and go back to the house, when she saw the tin trunk under Sam's workbench. She remembered how oddly Sam had behaved before. On a sudden impulse, she pulled the trunk from beneath the bench and opened it.

This time it wasn't empty. Something round was in the bottom, wrapped in a sheet of her kitchen foil. She smiled in satisfaction and set about unwrapping it. With the kitchen foil removed, she saw a dull green globe, made of something heavy and smooth. It was about the size of a football. She popped it back inside and began to drag the trunk back to the house. Once she had the trunk in the cottage's tiny sitting-room, she opened it again. The globe began to glow softly. Then it started to pulse with light. The pulsing increased in brightness and intensity until the globe was flashing rhythmically. Meg leaned forward, staring at it as if hypnotised.

In the woods a waiting Auton came to life. It swung its body from side to side, searching for the direction of the signal. Then it began to move forward, heading straight for the cottage.

In the security area of the plastics factory a light flashed on a monitor panel. The light flashed in exactly the same pulsing rhythm as the globe. Channing and Hibbert stood watching.

'Less than two miles away,' said Channing with satisfaction. 'We have found the swarm leader at last.'

'Aren't you going to collect it?' asked Hibbert.

'That is already being done.' Channing's eyes narrowed. His consciousness was linked to that of the Auton. He could see what it saw, hear what it heard. 'There – that little building. That is where the swarm leader is being held!' Channing's voice was exultant. He stood rigid and motionless, as if in a trance. Hibbert looked at him in horrified fascination. Channing said softly: 'We are nearly there.' His eyes stared blankly into the distance.

The Auton continued its relentless progress. In the distance it saw the cottage appear through the trees.

Meg suddenly shook her head, as if freeing herself from the hypnotic influence of the glowing sphere. Suddenly she slammed shut the lid, cutting off the flashing light. Then she began to drag the trunk out of the sitting-room. Let Sam keep the nasty thing in the shed if he wanted to, decided Meg. She wasn't going to have it in *her* house.

*

As the speeding UNIT car reached the edge of the woods, the Brigadier told the driver: 'Take us to the Command Post first. I'll let Captain Munro know we're here; see if there's any news.'

In the back seat of the car sat Liz, the Doctor and Ransome. Ransome had become increasingly silent as they came nearer to the scene of his terrifying experience.

Liz gave him an encouraging pat on the arm. 'No need to worry, this time, Mr Ransome,' she said. 'You won't be going back alone. The Brigadier can pick up some troops to go with us.'

Ransome looked ashamed. 'I'm beginning to think I can't face going back at all,' he confessed. 'I thought I was going to be all right, now, but it all seems to be coming back to me. It's as if they were still watching me.' There was the sound of panic in his voice.

The car was jolting down the forest track now, and they saw the tent with the UNIT sentry outside. The car came to a halt, the sentry saluted and Munro emerged from the tent.

Before the Brigadier could say anything, Munro spoke excitedly. 'This is marvellous, sir, you've turned up just in time. I've got a chap in here who actually found one of the meteorites. A whole one. He's been keeping it in a trunk in his shed!'

Sam Seeley was somewhat taken aback when a whole group of people poured into the tent. His eyes widened when he saw the Doctor. But Sam made no mention of having seen the arrival of the TARDIS. He reckoned he was in enough trouble. Anyway, who'd believe him? This tall chap was one of the nobs. When Sam, rather shamefaced, had told his story again, the Brigadier snapped: 'Captain

Munro, do you know where this man's cottage is?'

Munro turned to an Ordnance Survey map spread out on the table. 'It's here, sir. Just a few minutes away.'

'Right, you'd better come with us.'

Liz noticed Ransome. He'd followed them from the car, and was hanging about on the edge of the group, looking completely confused. 'Perhaps I could wait here,' he said.

Munro noticed Ransome for the first time. 'Yes of course. My chaps will look after you. Sergeant, get Mr Ransome some tea.'

Munro grabbed Sam by the arm. 'Come along, man. We need you to show us where the thing is.'

Munro and the Brigadier crammed into the front seat of the car, next to the driver, while Liz, the Doctor and Sam Seeley sat in the back. The car jolted off down the track, heading for the road.

Sam looked round approvingly at the padded comfort of the Brigadier's staff car. 'Very kind of you gentlemen to give me a lift home,' he said amiably. 'Beats riding my old bike.' Nobody answered, and Sam fell silent.

The cottage that they were making for stood still and silent. An Auton stepped from the forest and walked towards the cottage gate. Barney was still stretched out in the little front garden. He raised his head and growled at the approaching figure.

In the shed at the end of the garden Meg gave the trunk a final shove back under the workbench and stood up, dusting her hands. She stopped a moment, listening. How silent everything had become. Even the birds seemed to have stopped singing. From the house came the long drawn out howl of a dog.

Meg yelled: 'Barney, just you stop that racket.'

The dog howled again, on a rising note of terror. Uneasy, Meg moved towards the house. 'Just you shut up that racket now, Barney.'

There was yet another howl, cut short by a sudden yelp. Then silence. Meg stood listening for what seemed ages. Suddenly she heard the sound of smashing glass and splintering wood. Meg ran towards the house. She came into the little parlour and stopped in amazement.

The little room was a complete wreck. Chairs and table were broken, a dresser smashed open. A giant figure, its back turned, was rooting through the contents of a corner cupboard, searching with a sort of savage ferocity.

Meg was too indignant at the total wreck of her home to feel frightened. 'Hey, you!' she yelled. 'What you think you're at, then? Just you get out of here!'

The figure swung round and looked at her, and Meg gave a gasp of terror. The face was blank and smooth, the features crude and lumpy.

Meg whispered hoarsely: 'Now just you get out. My husband's about, you know.' But she knew as she spoke that the creature couldn't hear or understand her. Slowly she backed away. Then turning she ran through the little passage and out of the back door. Snatching the key from the lock, she closed the door and locked it from the outside. Then she ran down the garden path to Sam's shed.

Sam's old shotgun was in its usual place, hanging above the shed door. She grabbed it and broke it open.

There was a shattering crash from the house. Meg looked up. The back door had been burst completely from its hinges. Framed in the doorway, stood the Auton. For a moment it just stood there, watching her. Then it started to walk down the garden path. Meg raised the gun and pulled the trigger. There was a dry click. Of course. Sam never left the gun loaded. Meg searched frantically on the shelf by the shed door and found an open box of cartridges. With trembling hands, she broke open the gun and loaded it. Snapping the gun shut, she looked up. The Auton was almost upon her.

She levelled the gun. 'Now, you saw me load it,' she said shakily. 'You get away from here or I'll blow a hole in you.' The Auton continued to advance.

'I mean it! I'm not fooling, you know.' The Auton was almost within arm's length now. Meg raised the shotgun and fired, first one barrel and then the other. The Auton was rocked backwards by the blast. It recoiled a few paces, and Meg could see the smoking holes in the breast of its rough overalls. Then it began to walk forward again. There was no change in the expression of the blank face. Meg screamed once more. Then she fainted. The Auton stepped over her and went into the shed.

Channing's face was a mask of fierce concentration. He hissed: 'The signal is muffled but it is near now. It is very near. We must find it. We must find it.'

Everything was quiet as the Brigadier's staff car drew up outside the little cottage. Everyone climbed out of the car and Sam led the way inside.

'Meg!' he called. 'Meg, we got company.' He stopped appalled as he saw the wreckage all round him.

'I think we may be too late,' said the Doctor. Suddenly they heard a bumping noise from the garden. The Brigadier and Munro drew their revolvers. Followed by the others, they ran through the wrecked cottage and out of the shattered back door.

Meg's body lay crumpled at the side of the shed. The Auton was carrying the tin trunk up the path. Before anyone could stop him, Sam Seeley pushed his way to Meg's side. Ignoring the Auton, he picked up his wife and began carrying her out of danger. The Auton looked up, seeming to sense that it was watched. It dropped the trunk and raised an arm, pointing at the Brigadier. The hand dropped on its hinge. A nozzle appeared, projecting from the wrist.

'Down!' yelled the Doctor. 'Everybody down!' He gave the Brigadier and Munro a shove, grabbed Liz and hurled her back inside the building.

An energy-bolt sizzled over the Brigadier's head, blasting a hole in the brick wall of the cottage. The Brigadier and Munro took cover, Munro behind a coal bunker, the Brigadier round the angle of the wall. Both opened fire at once with their heavy service revolvers. The Auton reeled and staggered under the impact of the bullets, but it continued to return the fire, sending bolt after bolt of energy from its wrist-gun.

From his position in the doorway, the Doctor yelled: 'Brigadier, Captain Munro! Hold your fire!' The guns became silent. The Auton too stopped firing, moving its gun slowly from side to side. Speaking clearly and distinctly the Doctor called: 'The platoon must be nearly here. We'll capture it when they arrive.'

In the plastics factory Channing's face twisted with anger. 'Recall,' he hissed. 'Recall, recall!'

At his elbow Hibbert said nervously, 'What's happening?'

Channing said: 'UNIT. Too many of them. It is too soon for a pitched battle.'

At the cottage the little group watched in amazement as the Auton wheeled suddenly and made off through the woods. The Brigadier moved as if to pursue, but the Doctor stopped him. 'Let it go, Brigadier. If you caught it, you couldn't harm it. And it would certainly kill you.'

'What's all this about a relief platoon, Doctor? I didn't order any troops to follow us.'

The Doctor smiled. 'You and I know that. But *it* didn't.' He gestured in the direction of the Auton's retreat.

'You think that thing actually understood you?'

'Maybe not the thing itself. I think it was just a sort of walking weapon. But whoever is controlling it understood me.'

Forestalling any more questions, the Doctor said: 'Now let's take a look at what it came for.'

The Brigadier looked at Liz, who was helping Sam to revive Mrs Seeley. 'How is she?'

'Just shock, I think. We ought to get her to hospital.'

The Brigadier said: 'Munro, call an ambulance!'

As Mrs Seeley was helped inside the cottage, Sam said: 'I'll want compensation! Look at all this damage! And what about my reward?'

Exasperated, the Brigadier turned on him. 'By making off with that meteorite, Mr Seeley, you brought all of this upon yourself, and gravely hampered my investigations. As for a reward – you and your wife are both still alive and relatively unharmed. Isn't that reward enough?'

Chastened, Sam followed the Brigadier into the cottage. After all, he thought hopefully, there was always the newspapers. A story like his ought to be worth a bob or two. Sam could already see the headlines – 'MY STRUGGLE WITH THE MONSTER'. Still scheming hopefully, he followed the Brigadier into the cottage.

Liz joined the Doctor who was peering into the trunk. 'Fascinating!' he said. 'Quite fascinating. I was right about the size and shape, you see.'

Liz looked at the sphere. It was still pulsing, though now in a more subdued rhythm. The Doctor indicated the silver foil at the bottom of the trunk. 'He'd got it wrapped in this, you see. Aluminium foil. That, and the metal of the trunk, must have muffled the signals.'

'And when that poor woman took it out, it started calling for help! Hadn't you better wrap it up again?'

Deftly, the Doctor began to wrap the sphere in the kitchen foil. 'I think perhaps you're right.'

'Suppose the thing explodes, like the other one?'

The Doctor closed the lid of the trunk. 'There's no reason why it should, if we treat it gently. That is, unless it's got a built-in self-destruct impulse. Still, we'll just have to risk that.' And he beamed cheerfully at Liz.

'Doctor,' said Liz, 'you'll have to unwrap that thing and take it out of the trunk if we're going to work on it in the laboratory.'

'Yes, of course we will.' The Doctor swung the trunk onto his shoulder and started to carry it towards the car.

'Well,' said Liz, 'what do we do if that thing decides to come back and get it?'

The Doctor chuckled. 'That, my dear, is a very good question.'

Munro came out of the cottage. 'The ambulance is here, sir. Seeley's going with his wife to the hospital.'

The Brigadier nodded, and turned to the Doctor. 'Well, Doctor? What do we do now?'

It was curious, thought Liz, how the Doctor seemed to have assumed command. Or maybe it wasn't strange, she thought. There was something very reassuring about the Doctor.

He rubbed his chin thoughtfully. 'Well, it's pretty obvious where that creature came from. Obviously something very similar attacked Ransome at the plastics factory.'

'Right,' said the Brigadier crisply. 'I'll move in at once.'

The Doctor shook his head. 'And maybe face an army of those creatures? Until we know a little more about what's going on, we'd better move cautiously.'

'Then what do we do?'

The Doctor said: 'First we send this trunk back to UNIT H.Q., under armed guard.'

Munro stepped forward. 'I'll see to it right away, Doctor.'

'Mind,' said the Doctor warningly, 'no one's to open that trunk until I arrive.'

'I doubt if anyone will want to!' said Munro.

The Doctor turned to the Brigadier. 'Now I think we should collect Mr Ransome from your Command Post, and pay a nice friendly visit to that plastics factory.'

Channing paced up and down in silent fury. 'We must recover the swarm leader,' he said angrily.

'But if UNIT has taken it – and you don't want a pitched battle yet – how can we?' said Hibbert.

Channing said: 'There are other methods.' Suddenly he noticed the monitor screen. Ransome's brain-print pattern had reappeared and was pulsing brightly. Channing said with savage satisfaction: 'Your friend Ransome has been unwise enough to return to the area. Him at least we can deal with now!'

Alone in the UNIT Command Tent, Ransome swigged the last of his mug of now-cold tea. He was feeling tired and depressed. The idea of re-visiting the plastics factory terrified him, even with the prospect of the Brigadier's protection. And now he'd just been dumped here and left while they all rushed off somewhere hunting meteorites. Still at least he was safe for the moment. Ransome could hear the soldiers moving about in the clearing outside, and the bark of the Sergeant's voice as he supervised the unloading of stores from an army truck. Ransome was bored. He wished that the Sergeant would come back, so he'd have someone to talk to.

Something bumped against the canvas at the back of the tent. Ransome looked up idly, assuming that one of the soldiers had brushed against it. Then to his amazement a long rip appeared in the canvas wall. A figure stepped through it. Ransome leaped to his feet in utter terror. Facing him was an Auton.

Before Ransome could even scream, the hand dropped back on its hinge and a searing bolt of energy smashed him to the ground. The Auton trained its gun on the body and a beam of bright light shot from the wrist-gun. Ransome's body glowed red then white, and then simply vanished. The Auton stepped through the rip in the canvas as silently as it had come.

Minutes later the Brigadier's car drew up at the Command Post. Munro gave orders for sending the trunk to UNIT

H.Q. The Doctor, Liz Shaw and the Brigadier entered the tent. They looked round in puzzlement.

The Brigadier yelled: 'Sergeant! Where's Mr Ransome gone to?' The Sergeant appeared in the tent doorway.

'Nowhere, sir, not as far as I know. I left him in here drinking tea. I had to go out and get the supply truck unloaded.'

The Doctor was looking swiftly round the tent. Almost at once he spotted the slash in the tent wall.

'We can only presume he got out this way.'

'But why?' asked the Brigadier aggrievedly. 'Why should the chap just slope off like that?'

'He was pretty scared about the idea of going back to that factory,' Liz said thoughtfully. 'Maybe he decided he just couldn't face it.'

The Doctor moved away from the tent wall. 'We're all assuming he got out. Maybe something else got in.'

'Somebody kidnapped him – from my Command Post?' The Brigadier was appalled at the very thought.

The Doctor shrugged. 'After all, Ransome's story was our only link with the factory. If Mr Ransome's anywhere, that's where he'll be.'

As the car sped towards the factory, the Doctor sat chin in his hands, brooding. Liz sensed that his mind was turning over all that had happened, trying to find a pattern, a reason. He was still silent as they drove through the open gates, with the sign 'Auto Plastics' on them.

'They don't seem to object to visitors,' said Liz as they got out of the car.

'No, they wouldn't,' said the Doctor absently. 'They'd want to keep everything looking fairly normal. Right up till the last moment, that is.'

Liz looked at him curiously, but by now they were in the luxuriously furnished reception. The Brigadier explained his business to the pretty, rather doll-like girl receptionist. He was obviously prepared to over-ride all opposition. But there wasn't any.

'Mr Hibbert will see you now,' said the receptionist in her clear emotionless voice. 'Will you come this way please?' It was almost as if they'd had an appointment, thought Liz. As if they'd been expected.

She looked round curiously as they crossed the deserted factory floor. This was very advanced machinery, fully automated.

The Brigadier stopped for a moment, looking over his shoulder. Liz followed his gaze, and thought she saw someone moving behind one of the machines. Then the Brigadier murmured an apology, and they moved on. The girl took them up to the staircase that led to Hibbert's office, showed them inside, and silently withdrew.

Liz looked curiously at George Hibbert as he rose from behind his desk. He looked very like the average business executive anywhere. Dark striped suit, horn-rimmed glasses, greying hair. There were lines of strain and worry on the face, but no more than on the faces of many other businessmen.

Hibbert settled them all in chairs and then sat down behind his desk. He listened politely as the Brigadier introduced Liz and the Doctor, and explained the reason for their visit. The Brigadier gave a brief summary of the story Ransome had told them. His voice tailed away rather as he came to the end of it.

'And – er – well, there you are. You will appreciate that

extraordinary as the story is, we have to check on it.'

Hibbert looked politely puzzled. 'Well, if you say so, Brigadier. Though I would have thought that it was more a matter for a psychiatrist than a security man.'

'You mean that Ransome was unbalanced?'

'That, or simply malicious.'

Liz said: 'So there was no truth in this story at all?'

'Well, there was some. It's true that he used to work for me. It's also true that he designed a new type of electronic doll. It was a brilliant invention but far too complex and expensive for the mass-market. When I refused to produce it here, he went off to America in a huff to try and find backing.'

'And succeeded apparently,' cut in the Brigadier.

'So he told me. But the fact that others were prepared to risk their money didn't mean that I was prepared to risk mine. My attitude hadn't changed and I told him so. He seemed to feel I'd let him down. He became violently abusive and I had to ask him to leave.'

'So you think he made up this whole story just to cause you trouble?'

'I'm afraid so, Brigadier.'

'But why should he tell such a fantastic story?'

Hibbert shrugged. 'Why don't you ask him? I'd very much like to ask him that myself.'

'We were going to bring him with us,' said Liz. 'Unfortunately he disappeared before we set off.'

'I'm not surprised! Didn't dare to repeat all this nonsense to my face.'

The Doctor spoke for the first time. 'What exactly do you make in this factory, Mr Hibbert?'

'I'd be delighted to show you. Perhaps you'd care to have

a look at our store-rooms?'

The first room Hibbert took them to was lined with shelf after shelf of plastic dolls. Dolls with hair of every colour, dolls of every shape and size. Row upon row of china-blue eyes gazed at them unwinkingly from shiny pink plastic faces. Liz shivered. Somehow there was something rather sinister about so many of the little creatures in one place.

Hibbert waved his arm in a sweeping gesture. 'This was our original line, of course. However, since then we've broken into new territory. If you'd come through here.'

He took them into another, larger store-room. It seemed to be full of a huge crowd of silent figures, standing and waiting. Hibbert switched on a light.

'This is our big success at the moment. Display mannequins for department stores and shop windows.'

Liz looked round. Row after row of impossibly handsome men and beautiful women. If possible, they were even more sinister than the dolls.

The Doctor said: 'And do these, er... mannequins move?' Hibbert smiled. 'Of course they do.' He went up to the nearest mannequin and shifted its position. Arms and legs and body moved easily, and stayed as they were put.

'It's fortunate you came today. These will all be gone by tomorrow.' Hibbert put the mannequin back in its place. 'As you can see,' he said proudly, 'they're extremely supple and flexible. But I can assure you they don't move by themselves. We call them Autons, after the name of the factory – "Auto Plastics".'

The Brigadier coughed. 'Most impressive. Well, we mustn't take up any more of your time, Mr Hibbert.'

As Hibbert led them back across the factory floor towards the reception area, the Doctor asked: 'These Autons of yours – they're selling well?'

Hibbert nodded proudly. 'You'll find our Autons in every big department store in every city in England.'

Suddenly the Doctor stopped. He pointed across the factory floor to the area marked 'Restricted Zone'. 'I don't believe you've shown us what goes on in there, Mr Hibbert?'

'And I'm afraid I can't.' Hibbert turned to the Brigadier. 'Confidentially, Brigadier, we do a certain amount of work for the Ministry of Technology. Research into heat-resistant plastic for the space programme. Unless you and your party have special Ministry passes…' Hibbert shrugged apologetically. 'Well, I'm sure you, more than most people, will appreciate the necessity for good security.'

'And if I should get hold of a Ministry pass and come back here?'

'Then I'd be more than happy to show you the Research Laboratory. Though, mind you, I don't understand half of what's in there myself. My partner, Mr Channing, handles that side of our work.'

The Brigadier said: 'It's a pity we didn't get a chance to meet him.'

'Yes, indeed,' agreed Hibbert. 'Unfortunately he's away on a buying trip at the moment.' By now they were back in the reception area. Hibbert said: 'Well, if there's nothing more, gentlemen?'

The Brigadier glanced at the Doctor, who gave an almost imperceptible shake of his head.

'No, I don't think so,' said the Brigadier. 'Thank you for all your help. I hope we won't have to trouble you again.'

Hibbert said: 'Goodbye, Brigadier, Miss Shaw, Doctor. Let me know if I can be of any further assistance.' He watched as the three visitors got into the car and were driven away.

Hibbert turned and walked back into the factory area. Suddenly he seemed to sag, as if exhausted after some mighty effort. Channing appeared from behind the machinery and stood beside him.

'One of the visitors puzzled me. His brain was more powerful than most humans.'

Hibbert said: 'You mean the Scientific Adviser? Probably an exceptionally intelligent chap.'

'You did well, Hibbert. You did very well.'

'Do you think they were satisfied?'

'They are still suspicious. But they have no proof. It will take them time to move against us.'

'If they're not satisfied, they'll come back with more soldiers. They'll search in there.' Hibbert glanced towards the restricted zone.

'We have a way to stop them,' Channing reminded him. 'All we need is a short delay. When the time comes, no amount of soldiers will help them.'

The two of them began to walk towards the Replica Room.

As the staff car sped back towards London the Brigadier was saying: 'Well, that's the place all right. I caught a glimpse of someone skulking about on the factory floor. It was the chap who tried to kidnap you, Doctor.'

The Doctor nodded. 'Caught a glimpse of him myself. The elusive Mr Channing, no doubt. Yes, I think that creature at the cottage was one of their Autons.'

Liz asked: 'What are you going to do now?'

The Brigadier was decisive. 'Move in in force. Put a

cordon of troops round the factory, then search the place from top to bottom.'

'Suppose it's full of Autons – like the one that attacked us at the cottage?'

The Brigadier snorted. 'Well, revolver bullets didn't bother that thing much. But we'll see if they can laugh off bazookas or light artillery. Dammit, I'll bomb the place if I have to!'

The Brigadier's moustache positively bristled with military fervour. 'Old Scobie promised me full co-operation,' he went on, 'and I'm going to take him up on it.'

'Why do you have to go to him?' asked Liz.

'UNIT itself only maintains a small token force,' the Brigadier explained. 'For any really big operation we have to ask the Regulars for help.'

Liz turned to the Doctor who was slumped deep in his corner, chin in hands. 'You're very quiet, Doctor. Do you think the Brigadier should invade in force?'

The Doctor looked up. 'Wheel in your big guns by all means, Brigadier. We must close that factory just as soon as we can.'

'Then what are you looking so worried about?' asked Liz.

The Doctor sighed. 'I think we may be underestimating our enemy,' he said. 'Something tells me it isn't going to be so simple.' And he relapsed into silence.

As soon as they were back at UNIT H.Q., the Doctor seemed to revive. The tin trunk was waiting for them at the laboratory, and the Doctor immediately set about rigging up a complicated set of aerials and dials around it.

'To jam its signals,' he explained. Then he carefully took the globe and unwrapped it, fixing it on a specially rigged-up stand. At once the globe began to pulse angrily.

'No good having a tantrum, old chap,' the Doctor told it reprovingly. 'You'll just have to talk to *us*.'

'What do we do with it now?' asked Liz. 'Sit and admire it?'

'Didn't you hear what I said?' asked the Doctor. 'We're going to try and communicate with it. And test its strength.'

The Brigadier meanwhile was talking to General Scobie on the telephone. He told him all that had happened: the attack at the cottage, Ransome's disappearance, the visit to the plastics factory. Scobie was baffled, but co-operative.

'Auto Plastics,' he said incredulously. 'I was down there myself earlier today,' and rather diffidently he explained about the replica of him that was being made. 'Still,' he went on, 'that's neither here nor there. You can bank on me for all the co-operation you need.' The General glanced at his watch. 'It'll take a bit of time to set up, though. Tell you what, Lethbridge-Stewart, I'll get cracking right away. I can set up the mobilisation overnight, and we'll move in first thing tomorrow.'

'Couldn't be better, sir. Thank you again,' said the Brigadier.

'Right,' said Scobie, 'I'll be in touch with you about liaison. Good night, Brigadier.'

Scobie put down the 'phone and sighed. Extraordinary business. Still that's what the Brigadier and his chaps were for, to deal with things like this. Scobie had a flash of regret for the days when soldiering was simpler. A nice straightforward cavalry charge, now! Nothing to beat it. He was just about to pick up the 'phone and call his H.Q., when the doorbell rang.

General Scobie heaved an exasperated sigh. He'd been looking forward to a quiet evening with his collection of regimental memoirs. Who the devil could this be?

Scobie went to the door of the little mews flat and opened it. At the sight of the figure facing him, he fell back in horrified disbelief. Another General Scobie stood there looking at him impassively. As his other self bore down on him, he took a faltering step backward. The other General Scobie stepped after him. Channing appeared behind the second Scobie. 'Good evening, General,' he said. 'As I promised, I have brought your replica to see you.'

Channing and the second Scobie stepped into the flat, pushing the General before them. The door closed. There was a muffled, gurgling scream, and then silence.

9

The Creatures in the Waxworks

Full of his plans for the coming attack, the Brigadier burst into the laboratory.

'Well, I've fixed it all up,' he began cheerfully. 'We're moving in—'

'Ssh!' said Liz, waving him into silence.

Rather hurt, the Brigadier subsided. He stood watching as Liz and the Doctor surrounded the meteorite, or whatever the thing was, with a variety of complicated looking apparatus.

'All right, my dear, is the oscillator connected?' said the Doctor.

Liz was fitting two complex pieces of circuitry together.

'Hang on… yes, okay now.'

'Right. Switch on. I'll watch the graph.'

Liz flicked a switch and then turned a control knob. The apparatus began to give out a low hum.

The Brigadier looked at Liz and the Doctor as they bent over their instruments. He sighed, recognising that he hadn't a hope of understanding what they were up to. No doubt they'd tell him when it suited them. And *he* was supposed to be the one in command! Not for the first time the Brigadier considered applying for a transfer back to normal regimental duties. Life had been so simple then.

Parades, inspections, manoeuvres, more parades... He'd been offered the UNIT job not long after that Yeti business in the Underground. Presumably because he was the only senior British officer with experience in dealing with alien life forms. At the time it had seemed like a rather cushy number, carrying as it did the welcome promotion from Colonel to Brigadier. If only he'd known! First that nasty affair with the Cybermen, and now this. The trouble with the scientific approach, thought the Brigadier, was that it left you at the mercy of your scientists.

Then he brightened. For all their scientific mumbo-jumbo it was direct military action that was going to solve the problem. The Brigadier's eyes sparkled with anticipation at the thought of tomorrow's attack on the plastics factory.

Encouraged by this thought, he cleared his throat loudly and said: 'Perhaps you wouldn't mind telling me what you're actually trying to do, Doctor?'

The Doctor looked up. He gestured towards the green globe on its stand. The thing was now beginning to pulse angrily. 'Well, it appears that in there we have what one might loosely call a brain...' The Doctor took a quick look at the quivering needle that was drawing spidery lines on a recording graph. Fifty megacycles.'

Liz repeated: 'Fifty megacycles.' She turned the control knob a little further. 'Anything?' she asked.

The Doctor shook his head. 'No. Up another fifty, Liz.' As Liz adjusted her controls again, the Doctor resumed his explanation.

'You see, Brigadier, we know it's emitting a signal of some kind. So if we can establish the frequency on which it operates we may be able to counteract its – oh dear!'

While the Doctor had been speaking, the hum of the

120

apparatus had been rising steadily higher. There was a puff of smoke, and a shower of sparks shot from the apparatus. Hurriedly Liz switched off and stood back.

'I rather think we overloaded the circuit,' she said ruefully. She began to inspect the apparatus. 'Yes, look! The thermionic valve's blown.' Liz began to disconnect part of the apparatus.

'Now that really *is* interesting,' said the Doctor in a rather pleased tone. 'It means that there must be an extremely high resistance on the...'

The Brigadier interrupted hastily: 'Doctor, you say that thing is some kind of a brain?'

'Well, part of a brain. Or call it an intelligent entity. That's probably nearer the mark.'

'And it's signalling somewhere? Where to?'

The Doctor gave him that patient look again. 'To the rest of itself. Surely that's obvious?'

Liz looked up from her work on the apparatus. 'So the other globes that came down – they're all part of one entity? Some kind of collective intelligence?'

The Doctor nodded. The Brigadier peered at the globe with a kind of revulsion. He couldn't help feeling that it was peering back at him. 'Can it see us, or hear us?' he asked, instinctively dropping his voice to a whisper.

The Doctor chuckled. 'My dear chap, it isn't sentient.'

'Our measurements show that there's no physical substance inside it,' said Liz.

'Probably gaseous ions held in a hetero-polar bond. Or something like that,' said the Doctor, as if that made everything perfectly clear.

The Brigadier persisted. 'But it is alien – and dangerous?'

The Doctor looked at the globe thoughtfully. 'Well, it's an intelligent life form, and it isn't here by accident. I'm afraid we must assume that its intentions are hostile.'

'But if it has no physical form, how can it harm us?'

The Doctor said impatiently: 'Once here, it can presumably create for itself a physical form, or even a number of them. Otherwise there would have been no point in its coming.'

Liz said: 'A form like the thing at the cottage?'

'That's right. There may be other forms of it, too. Creatures we haven't even seen yet.'

Liz shuddered. 'I'm not sure that I want to.'

The wall 'phone buzzed and the Brigadier picked it up. He said: 'Yes? Ah, General Scobie... good, put him on.' He listened for a moment and then the familiar voice of Scobie came on the line.

'Lethbridge-Stewart? About this raid on the plastics factory. Not on, I'm afraid. They're doing important Government work, and they mustn't be interfered with.'

The Brigadier could hardly believe his ears. 'But, sir, our investigations all point to the fact that this factory is the centre...'

Scobie's voice cut in coldly: 'I'm sorry, Brigadier, but this is a direct order. Keep away from that factory, or you'll find yourself in very serious trouble. By the way, I'm recalling my men. They're urgently needed elsewhere.' There was a click and the 'phone went dead.

The Brigadier turned to the others, his face grim. 'That was General Scobie. He's cancelled the raid on the factory.' The Doctor and Liz were busily re-assembling their apparatus. The Doctor looked up.

'Well, you'll just have to go ahead without him, won't

you?'

'Go ahead? How can I, without any troops?'

'What about all those men you had searching the woods,' asked Liz.

'They were regular army chaps. On loan from General Scobie. Now he's withdrawn them all.'

The Brigadier began to pace the laboratory. 'Well, I'll just have to go over his head. Get on to the Home Secretary. Make him revoke the order. If that doesn't work, I can get on to UNIT H.Q., in Geneva, and ask them to put pressure on the Government.'

The Doctor's face was grave. 'All that's going to take time – and I've suddenly got a nasty feeling that time's running out on us.'

'How do you think the plastics factory people managed to get Scobie to change his mind?' asked Liz. 'Have they got influence in high places?'

'No idea,' said the Brigadier disgustedly. 'Unless they managed to appeal to his vanity with that replica business.'

The Doctor looked up keenly. 'Replica? What replica? Why didn't you tell me?'

'Didn't give me much chance, did you?' said the Brigadier aggrievedly. 'Only just heard about it myself.'

He told them about Scobie's earlier visit to the factory. About the special exhibition of VIPs that was being held at a famous London waxworks.

The Doctor's face lit up. 'A waxworks. My goodness, a waxworks. Yes, of course!' He glanced at the clock. 'Come on, Liz, we might just get there before they close.' Almost dragging Liz after him, the Doctor rushed from the laboratory.

'Hey, wait! Just a moment,' the Brigadier called after

them. Then he shrugged his shoulders. Let them go to the waxworks. Let them go to the Tower of London, Buckingham Palace and the London Zoo while they were at it! And much good might it do them. As usual all the real work was left to him. Like children, these scientists!

The Brigadier gave the glowing green sphere a final disgusted glare. Malignantly, it flashed back at him. Then he left the laboratory and went down the corridor to his office. Throwing himself into his chair, he snatched up the 'phone.

'Operator, this is Brigadier Lethbridge-Stewart. Get me the Home Secretary on the security line. I want to fix up an immediate appointment.'

Liz Shaw hung on to her seat as the Doctor raced the UNIT jeep through the London traffic. He'd only been dissuaded from taking Mr Beavis's Rolls by her reminder that it was probably on the stolen cars list. But he was getting quite a turn of speed out of the jeep.

'Nippy little things, these,' yelled the Doctor happily, as they took a corner on two wheels, outraging a passing traffic-warden.

'Doctor, please,' yelled Liz. 'What's the rush? And did you ever pass a driving-test?'

The Doctor was indignant. 'Of course I did! I'm a qualified rocket pilot on the Mars to Venus route. And as for the rush – if we can get to the waxworks before closing time, it'll save us the bother of breaking in!'

The Doctor whizzed the jeep through a narrowing gap between two heavy lorries. Liz shuddered and decided not to distract him with any more questions.

In a few minutes they arrived outside the waxworks.

With a fine disregard for regulations the Doctor parked the jeep on a double yellow line, and hared up the steps, Liz following behind. There was still ten minutes to go till closing time. Liz went to the ticket-box.

'Hardly worth going in now, is it?' said the old attendant at the main entrance, as Liz showed him the tickets.

The Doctor beamed at him. 'Well, as a matter of fact, old chap, we just wanted a very quick look at one particular exhibit – the special VIP room.'

The attendant seemed surprised. 'Don't get many asking for that, sir,' he said. 'Here, you come with me, I'll show you where it is.' Liz and the Doctor followed him along the corridors. Most of the visitors were going the other way, making for the exits. The old man took them to a small room, set apart from the main displays. There was the usual raised platform with a silk rope railing it off. On the platform stood a number of still figures. Most were of ordinary looking men and women in business clothes, though one or two were in uniform. Liz looked at the Doctor in puzzlement. Was this all they had come to see? But the Doctor was looking round with keen interest. Apart from themselves the room was completely empty.

'They don't seem very popular, do they?' he said cheerfully, turning to the old attendant.

'Well, between you and me sir, this lot aren't,' said the old man. 'It's choice of subject if you ask me. I mean, look at 'em.' He waved round the room. 'Top Civil Servants, one or two MPs, high-ranking blokes in the Army, Navy and Air Force, even the Police. All very important ladies and gentlemen, I'm sure. But – well, not a lot of glamour about them, you see. And the public must have glamour.' The little old man nodded his bald head emphatically.

'They do seem rather a dull lot,' agreed Liz.

'Mind you,' said the attendant loyally, 'this new modelling process is marvellous, no doubt about it. I mean, see for yourself. Looks real, even feels real. Every detail perfect. Now if only they'd done a few pop stars, or a decent murderer or two.'

'That wouldn't have been nearly so much use to them,' said the Doctor, almost to himself. Ignoring the attendant's startled look, he said: 'I gather these waxworks aren't made here – in fact, they're not really waxworks at all.'

'That's right, sir. Some factory down in the country do them. Completely new process. Some new kind of plastic.'

'How do they come to be on display here?' asked Liz.

The old man's voice became confidential. 'Well, you see, miss, these people are trying to break into the waxworks line. So they got on to us and offered to provide a whole display completely free, just to see how the things went with the public. This little room was empty, so we agreed. Between you and me, it hasn't been much of a success.'

'On the contrary,' said the Doctor, 'I think it's been a great success.' He gave the puzzled old man a charming smile. 'Is the display complete now?'

'Well, we thought it was. One more turned up today, though. That's him over there.'

He pointed to a stiff uniformed figure at the end of the room. Liz and the Doctor walked up to it.

'It's General Scobie!' said Liz.

'Just as I thought,' said the Doctor. He turned to the attendant. 'Thank you so much for being so helpful. We mustn't keep you any more. I know there's only a few more minutes, and you'll be busy closing up. We'll find our own way out.'

'Right you are, sir,' said the attendant. 'You'll find an exit just over there.' And he shuffled out of the room.

Liz turned back to the Doctor. 'What's so surprising about a replica of Scobie? We knew they'd done one.'

But the Doctor wasn't listening. To Liz's astonishment, he swung his long legs over the silk rope and climbed up on the platform. He began examining the model of General Scobie. He tweaked its ear, looked into its eyes, and finally first peered at, then listened to, the watch on the model's right wrist. Then he climbed back over the rope.

'Liz, if you were making a model of someone, would you put a wristwatch on it?'

'I might – if it had to look completely authentic.'

'All right. Would you also go to the trouble of winding the watch up and setting it to show the correct time and date?'

Liz looked at the model of Scobie, then back at the Doctor. 'I don't know,' she said uneasily. 'What are you getting at?'

The Doctor indicated the rows of silent figures. 'All these models must be taken into custody immediately. I'll want to examine them in the laboratory.'

'You can't arrest an entire waxworks display.'

'*I* can't, but the Brigadier can! Change for the telephone, please, Liz.' Urgently the Doctor held out his hand.

Liz fished out some change and gave it to him. With a muttered 'Back in a minute,' the Doctor rushed off.

Left alone with the silent models, Liz looked around her. She examined the replica of General Scobie. It did look uncannily lifelike. But surely the Doctor couldn't mean…? And what about all the others?

She looked up in relief as the Doctor came hurrying

back. 'Nobody there,' he said bitterly. 'The Brigadier's gone round to see the Home Secretary and young Munro's on his way back from Essex. Just some idiot soldier who'd never heard of me and didn't understand what I was talking about.'

'I'm not sure that *I* do,' said Liz. 'What do we do now?'

'If the Brigadier can't help us, we shall have to help ourselves.'

Liz looked at him with horror. 'You're not suggesting we just steal these things?'

'Well, not all of them,' said the Doctor reasonably. 'But we should be able to manage one or two little ones, surely?'

'And what will the staff say when we start walking off with the exhibits?'

The Doctor gave her a pitying look. 'We don't do it right now, Liz. We'll wait till the place is closed and empty.'

Liz drew a deep breath. 'Doctor, if you imagine for one moment…'

From outside in a corridor they heard an attendant's voice. 'Come along now please, ladies and gentlemen. The waxworks is now closed.'

The Doctor grabbed Liz by the hand. 'Come on, Liz. Hide!'

The old attendant came into the room and peered round shortsightedly. The place was empty. He wondered briefly about the strange couple who had been so interested in this display. Must have gone out by another exit, he thought. He turned out the lights and went back into the main corridor.

After a moment, two of the models in the rear rank moved and stirred. Cautiously Liz and the Doctor came

128

out of their stiff poses and climbed off the platform.

'Splendid,' said the Doctor. 'Now all we have to do is wait until things quieten down a bit.'

Liz sat down on the edge of the platform. 'Doctor, when you were talking about the watch – did you mean that's the *real* General Scobie?'

'Oh yes, I think so. Under some form of deep hypnosis, poor chap.'

'Can't you bring him out of it?'

The Doctor looked dubious. 'Too dangerous. I don't know the exact techniques they used, you see. It could do him permanent damage, even kill him, if things went wrong.' The rows of silent figures were now shadowed in the semi-darkness. 'What about this lot? Are they real people too?' said Liz nervously.

'Oh, I doubt it. You see, these replicas haven't been activated yet. They had to use their Scobie replica early.'

'So as to stop the Brigadier from attacking the factory?'

'Exactly.'

'And these others?'

'They'll be activated too. When the time comes. That's why I need to get some of them back to the lab. I've got the apparatus we fixed up for a weapon to use against them, you see. But I'll need to run proper tests.'

'How much longer have we got to wait here then? I keep getting the feeling those things are watching me.'

The Doctor gave her an encouraging pat on the back. 'Cheer up, it won't be for much longer. And it could be much worse, you know.'

'It could?

The Doctor smiled. 'Just think – we might be in the Chamber of Horrors.'

Channing and Hibbert stood silently, almost reverently, beside the huge tank. The creature inside was much bigger now. It could be seen moving and struggling with restless life, as if ready to break out.

Channing adjusted more controls to speed up the flow of nutrient. Hibbert asked in a kind of fascinated horror: 'What will it look like when it is ready?'

Channing straightened up from the controls and looked at him impassively. 'I cannot tell you that.'

'But you must know,' protested Hibbert. 'You made it.'

'I made nothing. I merely created an environment which enabled the energy units to create the perfect life form.'

Hibbert rubbed his forehead. 'Perfect for what?'

'For the conquest of this planet,' said Channing coldly.

Hibbert's face twisted with effort. 'I don't under—'

Channing looked at him with sudden contempt. 'Of course you don't understand. How could you?'

Hibbert backed away in terror. Channing forced himself to remember that he would need this weak human tool for just a little longer.

'Don't struggle against me, Hibbert,' he said soothingly. 'Trust me. Obey me. We must work together.'

Hibbert relaxed. 'Yes, of course. It's all so clear when I'm with you. It's just that sometimes…' Hibbert shook his head as if to clear it. When he spoke again his voice was bright and cheerful. He might have been any business executive discussing a routine problem with a colleague.

'What about the swarm leader? It still has to be recovered from UNIT.'

Channing's tone was equally matter of fact. 'That is being attended to now. By *our* General Scobie.'

'But he's only a copy. If he's detected now...'

Confidently Channing said: 'Until now, Hibbert, you have seen only the basic Autons in action. Crude weapons with a single purpose – to kill. The facsimiles are perfect reproductions, even down to brain cells and memory traces.'

'There is still a difference. They're not human beings.'

'The only difference is the absence of emotion. And emotion is inefficient, Hibbert. That is why the Nestenes are your superiors.' Channing turned to go. 'I am going to activate the facsimiles. You will see then how effective they are.'

Captain Munro paced about indecisively. He was wishing he knew what the blazes was going on. First the Essex operation had been cancelled. All the army men on loan to UNIT had been suddenly recalled. The Major in charge of the withdrawal had been as puzzled as Munro himself. 'Sorry, old chap, direct orders from General Scobie himself. All these chaps are going on special training manoeuvres in Scotland.' Now, back at UNIT H.Q., Munro had learned from the duty corporal that a raid on the plastics factory had been suddenly mounted and as suddenly cancelled. The Brigadier was off trying to secure an interview with the Home Secretary, and the Doctor and Miss Shaw had vanished on some wild goose chase. Apparently the Doctor had 'phoned in some time ago with a wild demand that they should attack a waxworks. Then he'd run off in a huff without saying where he was speaking from. There didn't seem much that Munro could usefully do about anything.

Feeling baffled, lost and generally deserted, Munro decided that he might as well go home. After a night and a day combing those wretched woodlands he could do with a night in a proper bed. Yawning, Munro was just about to go and tell the duty corporal of his intention when he heard voices in the main area. To his astonishment he recognised the familiar tones of General Scobie. Hastily grabbing his cap, Munro dashed from his office. In the reception area he found General Scobie accompanied by two tough-looking armed military policemen. The thoroughly terrified duty corporal seemed to be protesting feebly about something.

Saluting, Munro said: 'Can I help you, sir?' As Scobie turned round Munro noticed that the old boy had none of his usual cheerfulness about him.

Scobie's voice was cold and formal. 'Ah, Munro. This fool here seems incapable of obeying a simple order.'

'I'm sorry to hear that, sir. What's the problem?'

'No problem. I'm taking the meteorite off UNIT's hands.'

'But surely, sir...' Munro protested.

'Where is it?' barked Scobie.

'In the laboratory, sir. But with respect...'

Scobie wasn't listening. Followed by the two military policemen, he marched down the corridor and into the lab. Munro had no choice but to follow.

In the laboratory the meteorite was still standing on its special stand. As Scobie entered the green globe began once more to pulse with light. Scobie looked at it with satisfaction and reached out to take it. Hurriedly Munro said: 'May I ask what you intend to do with it, sir?'

'The Government are sending it to the National Geophysical Laboratory.'

'The Doctor and Miss Shaw had already begun to run a series of tests—'

132

'And where's this precious Doctor now, eh?'

'I'm not quite sure, sir,' Munro admitted. 'But I'm sure he'll be back soon and so will the Brigadier. If the matter could wait till then…'

Scobie was insistent. 'Certainly not. This thing's too important to be left to some nameless eccentric.'

Again he reached for the meteorite but Munro managed to edge between Scobie and the stand.

'I'm sorry, sir, but I think the Brigadier ought to be informed. I've no authority to part with the meteorite.'

Suddenly Scobie's eyes seemed to blaze with anger. 'Are you refusing to obey an order, Captain Munro?' There was a cold ferocity in Scobie's voice as he went on: 'I am forced to remind you that, although you are attached to UNIT, you are still a serving officer in the British Army. Will you hand over that meteorite? Or must I take it – and have you placed under arrest on a charge of mutiny?'

Munro was silent for a moment. His every instinct told him that something was badly wrong. For one moment he considered resistance but the effect of years of military training was too strong. He said stiffly: 'You leave me no alternative, sir. But under protest.' He stepped back from the stand.

Carefully, almost reverently, Scobie lifted the pulsing globe from its stand. Followed by the two silent military policemen, he turned and strode from the laboratory.

The Doctor and Liz sat waiting in the semi-darkness. Liz's head nodded forward, and she realised that, in spite of her strange surroundings, she was almost asleep.

The Doctor rose to his feet, yawned and stretched. 'Come on, Liz. I think we've waited long enough. The place should be empty now.'

The silence was shattered by the banging open of a door in the distance. The sound of marching footsteps echoed along the empty corridors, coming towards their room.

'Oh yes?' whispered Liz. 'What's all that then?'

The footsteps were now almost at the door. Hurriedly the Doctor grabbed Liz's hand and dragged her to the back of the room, where a long velvet curtain covered a recessed window. They both slipped behind the curtain.

Light spilled into the room from the corridor, as the door was thrown open. Liz peered out through a tiny gap. Channing stood framed in the doorway. Beside him was Hibbert. And behind them stood two more dim figures. Liz saw that their features were crude and lumpy and the eyes blank. They were Autons, like the thing that had attacked them at the cottage. She could feel the Doctor's hand gripping her arm fiercely, warning her to keep absolutely still and silent.

Channing looked keenly round the room. It seemed as if his eyes could burn through the curtain to reveal their hiding-place.

Channing said suddenly: 'I sense the presence of human life forms in this room.'

Liz edged away from the curtain. She could feel the Doctor tense beside her. She heard Hibbert reply: 'There's only us here, and the facsimiles. And Scobie.'

Channing said: 'Yes, of course. Scobie.'

Then Hibbert's voice again: 'What must you do to activate them?'

'Do? Nothing. They know that it is time.'

Liz couldn't resist looking again through the tiny gap. The silent figures on the platform began to stir. Heads turned, hands and feet moved. Jerkily, hesitantly at first, the figures took a few stumbling paces. Then, seeming to gather confidence, they began to step down from the low platform. In the same eerie silence they marched one by one from the room. Soon only one figure was left. That of Scobie. The real Scobie, Liz reminded herself. Left all alone while his inhuman companions walked away.

'Where will they go?' she heard Hibbert ask.

There was an icy triumph in Channing's reply. 'To take their places. It is time for them to begin their work.'

Channing turned and followed the Replicas. Hibbert stood gazing for a moment into the empty room. Suddenly Liz realised with horror that his eyes were fixed on hers. Liz wondered if he had seen her through the gap in the curtains. Hibbert hesitated for a moment, then followed Channing from the room. The two faceless creatures followed behind him. The door closed.

Liz and the Doctor stepped out into the room. The Doctor said softly: 'We must warn the Brigadier at once! Their plans must be far more advanced than I'd realised.' Suddenly the door opened. They whirled round to face it. Hibbert was standing there. He was alone.

Slowly, hesitantly, he came towards them. He said in a thick, slurred voice: 'What are you doing here? You shouldn't be here. Channing... Channing will...'

The Doctor moved forward and spoke in a low urgent voice: 'Channing will kill us if you let him know we're here. He killed your friend Ransome.'

Hibbert's voice was confused. 'Ransome? I had to dismiss him. He had to be dismissed because... Channing said...'

The Doctor said in an urgent whisper: 'Channing is controlling your mind. You must resist him. Channing is your enemy. He's the enemy of the whole human race.'

Hibbert looked at him, in distress. 'Channing is my partner. There's a new policy, you see. It's because of the new policy.'

'Now listen to me, Hibbert,' said the Doctor firmly. 'You must get away from Channing. Get away from him and *think*. Come to UNIT. I can help you.'

Hibbert stared at him in anguish. He rubbed his hand over his eyes, shook his head as if trying to clear it. Suddenly there came the sound of echoing footsteps in the empty corridor. 'Remember,' hissed the Doctor, 'they'll kill us.'

Channing's voice called: 'Hibbert! Where are you, Hibbert?' Liz and the Doctor had just time to duck behind their curtain before Channing appeared in the doorway, an Auton behind him.

From the gap in the curtain Liz saw him look round

the room. 'What are you doing, Hibbert? Is anything the matter?'

Liz held her breath as Hibbert stared back at Channing. She could almost see the struggle in his mind between the effect of the Doctor's appeal and Hibbert's fear of Channing.

Hibbert said: 'No, nothing's wrong. I was just checking.'

'There is nothing to check. We are finished here. Come.' Channing turned and left the room. Hibbert gave a last glance at the velvet curtain, and obediently followed him. For a moment the Auton stood poised in the doorway as if surveying the room. Then it, too, turned and left.

Liz heard the sound of their retreating footsteps. There was a sudden crash as a door somewhere was slammed. Liz and the Doctor emerged cautiously from behind the curtain.

Liz said: 'Do you think he'll tell Channing we were here?'

The Doctor rubbed his chin. 'I hope not.'

'Why didn't he give us away?'

'Because Hibbert is still a human being,' said the Doctor. 'His mind is being dominated by Channing. But the human mind is a wonderfully resilient thing. It's almost impossible to control it completely for very long.'

Liz nodded in understanding. 'So his real personality keeps trying to break through?'

'That's right. And the control seems to be weakening. It's only completely effective when Channing's actually with him. If he can manage to get away from Channing completely, he may be able to shake off his influence.'

The Doctor listened at the door for a moment. 'They

seem to be all gone.'

Thankfully Liz followed him to the door. She couldn't get away from the place soon enough. She stopped in the doorway and looked back. General Scobie stood in solitary state on the now empty platform. 'What about him?'

The Doctor shot Scobie a regretful glance. 'Nothing we can do for him now. The poor old chap is safer where he is. Come on, Liz.'

They made for the nearest exit.

10

The Final Battle

As Liz and the Doctor approached the Brigadier's office, they heard his voice raised in outrage and astonishment. 'And you mean to say you simply stood there and let him walk off with it?'

They entered the room to find Munro standing unhappily to attention before the Brigadier's desk.

'There simply wasn't any alternative, sir. He *is* a General. Besides, he had two armed MPs with him. It was that, or find myself under arrest. And they'd have taken the globe anyway. I tried to contact you as soon as it happened, sir.'

The Brigadier waved Liz and the Doctor to chairs. 'The reason you couldn't contact me, Munro,' he said bitterly, 'was because I have been spending many long hours in the ante-rooms of Whitehall, trying to get in to see a number of important Government officials. With, I might add, a complete and utter lack of success. Either they were tied up in endless conferences, or they'd left early for a long weekend.' He turned to the Doctor and Liz. 'And I now get back here, only to learn that, not content with cancelling the operation, Scobie's turned up behind my back and walked off with the only piece of evidence.'

'Oh that wasn't Scobie, Brigadier,' said Liz. 'Scobie's still at the waxworks. That must have been his replica.'

'Exactly,' said the Doctor. 'They activated that one first

because they needed it to deal with UNIT. Now that the rest of them are on the loose, we're going to have *real* problems.'

The Brigadier gazed at them blankly. 'Others? What others? Will you kindly explain what you're talking about, Doctor?'

Briefly, the Doctor and Liz told of their discoveries at the waxworks. At the end of the story, the Brigadier scarcely looked any the wiser. 'Are you trying to tell me that some blessed waxwork walked in here and commandeered that globe?'

Munro said: 'His manner *was* very strange, sir. Sort of cold and inhuman. Not really like himself at all. But I'd never have thought...'

'Don't you see?' said the Doctor, 'that's the cunning of it. The Replicas aren't *exactly* the same as human beings. Nothing is. A wife, or a child, or a close friend could detect them in a moment. But we're not talking about personal relationships. We're talking about people in authority. Seniors giving orders to juniors.'

Liz joined in. 'After all, Brigadier, if *you* came in here all fierce and unfriendly, and started barking orders at everybody, I don't suppose anybody would notice the slightest...' Her voice tailed away as she realised what she was saying. Munro concealed a grin behind a sudden attack of coughing.

'All the same, she's quite right,' said the Doctor. 'A lot of the Replicas will probably cause some suspicion. But they'll all be able to achieve a great deal of damage before they're detected.'

'What harm?' said the Brigadier. 'What are these things *for*?'

Patiently the Doctor explained. 'Very soon they'll have taken over all the important positions in the country.'

'What about the originals, the real people?' asked the Brigadier.

'Some of them will have been got out of the way – like poor Scobie. The others, well…' The Doctor shrugged. 'A number of very important people will start appearing in two places at once, giving contradictory orders. It'll all add to the confusion when the invasion starts.'

'Invasion!'

'Don't tell me you hadn't realised, Brigadier. Everything that's happened so far has been just a preliminary. Before long the full-scale attack will begin.'

'What are we going to do about it?' said the Brigadier. 'I've tried to alert the Government, but no one will listen.'

The Doctor stood up. 'Two things, Brigadier,' he said decisively. 'First Miss Shaw and I must devise a weapon to use against the Autons. Once that is done, *you* must attack the plastics factory.'

'How can I? I keep telling you, Scobie's withdrawn all his men.'

The Doctor frowned. 'You must have *some* men available?'

'Myself, Munro, one or two headquarters staff…'

'Don't forget, there's Miss Shaw – and me!' The Doctor smiled encouragingly. 'Not much of an army, is it, Brigadier? But it'll have to do.'

The thing in the huge plastic coffin was almost complete now. It surged and pulsed, making the whole room vibrate. Channing stood watching it, with an air of quiet satisfaction. After a moment the door to the security area opened and

Scobie, or rather Scobie's Replica, joined him. In its hands the Replica carried the pulsing green globe. Channing turned. 'They suspected nothing?'

The Replica answered in the same flat emotionless voice. 'Nothing. The human soldiers accept my orders without question.'

'And what of UNIT?'

'UNIT is being watched. If they move against us, we shall know. And without their soldiers they are powerless. They will not dare to attack.'

'Humans are not totally predictable,' said Channing. 'It is growing harder to maintain my control over the man Hibbert. Now he has disappeared.'

'Hibbert is no longer necessary.'

'No.' There was satisfaction in Channing's voice. 'We need no one now.'

He took the energy unit from the hands of Scobie's Replica, and placed it carefully in a kind of incubator next to the great plastic coffin. The pulsing of the glowing green globe rose to a peak, as Channing pulled a series of controls. Then with a final flash of light the energy unit became inert. The fragment of the Nestene consciousness which it carried had been absorbed. The final element had been added. The Nestene Mind, that vast cosmic will and intelligence that linked Channing, the Replicas, the killer Autons and the handsome display mannequins in windows all over the country, was now complete.

Channing turned to the Replica, his eyes blazing with exultation.

'Tomorrow we will activate the Autons. This planet will soon be ours!'

*

A vast tangle of electronic equipment lay on the laboratory bench. Liz Shaw was helping the Doctor to connect and cross-connect a maze of circuitry.

'Let me see,' muttered the Doctor, grappling with a confusion of multi-coloured leads. 'A red and a yellow makes...'

'Green?' suggested Liz hopefully. 'Honestly, Doctor, I'd be a lot more help if I knew what this contraption of yours was supposed to do.'

The Doctor looked up. 'Oh, didn't I explain that? Well, you remember the device we were testing the green globe with – when we still had a globe to test?'

Liz nodded.

'Well, this is exactly the same sort of thing. With one or two refinements.'

'As I remember, Doctor,' said Liz, *that* thing fused.'

'Indeed it did,' admitted the Doctor. 'But this one is a good deal more powerful. This time I'm hoping that exactly the reverse will happen. The Auton will fuse!'

Liz watched him as he went on working tirelessly. The long nimble fingers deftly sorted out wires and the cross-connections, working quickly and surely.

Liz yawned. 'Couldn't we take a break, Doctor? I can hardly keep my eyes open.'

The Doctor shook his head. 'Must get finished, my dear.' He looked up at Liz and she saw the lines of tension in his face, the controlled worry in his eyes. 'I don't think there's very much more time, you see,' he said gently. 'We may need this device very soon.' The Doctor went on working and Liz yawned again. She looked out of the lab window. There were a few pale streaks of light in the sky. She looked at her watch. It would soon be morning.

'Just think,' she said, 'most of the rest of London is just starting the day!'

The city was coming to life. Office cleaners were leaving the towering blocks in chattering bands. Commissionaires and porters were reporting for duty. Shop managers and staff were letting themselves into their shops, getting ready to open the doors and face the public. The earliest of the office workers, and the keenest shoppers, were getting off their buses and emerging from Underground stations. Soon a normal, bustling London day would be in full swing. But this day, in London, and in cities all over the country, was to be like no other. This was the morning of the Auton invasion.

In the shop windows and in the department stores the mannequins stood waiting. A policeman patrolling along Oxford Street cast a casual eye at the window display in one of the big stores. A group of window dummies, dressed in bright, casual sports clothes, sat under a beach umbrella in a cheerful seaside setting. The policeman thought longingly of his own holidays. Only another two weeks... As he passed on his way the mannequins posing round the table stirred and came to life. Jerkily at first, they rose from their beach chairs and rugs. The tallest raised its hand in a pointing gesture. The hand dropped away on its hinge to reveal a gun nozzle. The rest of the dummies in the group followed suit. For all their handsome faces and bright holiday clothes, these, too, were killer Autons. Swiftly, unhesitatingly, their leader stepped straight through the store window and out onto the pavement.

The astonished policeman heard the crash of glass and spun round. His first thought was that there must have been some sort of accident. He stopped in utter amazement at the sight of the tall figure of the Auton stalking towards him along the pavement. Other figures followed the first Auton through the gap, stepping onto the pavement. From up and down the street came the crash of glass as other Autons came to life. The policeman's next thought was of some kind of enormous hoax. Students, he thought vaguely. They'd gone too far this time. That thought was also his last. As he ran towards the group of Autons, their leader raised its wrist-gun and blasted him to the ground.

By now other groups of Autons were appearing on the pavement. Ruthlessly they blasted down everyone they met. People ran screaming, trying to escape. In streets nearby, in streets all over London, and in the streets of every major city in Britain, it was the same story. People screamed and panicked and ran, and the Autons blasted them down.

The police received thousands upon thousands of calls. But there was little they could do. Arms were issued, but the few rifles and revolvers available were powerless against the Autons. BBC and ITV issued urgent warnings. 'Don't go to work. Don't go out shopping. Stay indoors and barricade yourselves in your homes. Admit no one you do not know.'

Many people were saved by warnings like these, but many others, already out on the streets, were unable to escape. The Autons seemed to be everywhere.

The Government declared martial law and called out the Army. But most of the available troops were mysteriously absent on manoeuvres far away from the big towns. They were recalled at once, but things seemed to go wrong continually. Orders failed to arrive, or were misinterpreted. Troops were told to stay put, or sent to the wrong place. In the other services the story was the same. The Navy and the Air Force armed what men they could, but the men never seemed to get clear orders, or to arrive where they were wanted. It was as though in every position of authority traitors were working against the Government, deliberately confusing the situation.

In an office in Whitehall a young civil servant listened appalled as he heard his Minister on the telephone, deliberately giving orders that would worsen the situation. He rushed into the office to demand an explanation. The Minister stretched out his hand in a curious pointing gesture – and the hand dropped away to reveal a gun.

There were many other similar scenes. Many more of the Replicas were detected, but not before they had done enormous damage, spreading chaos and confusion everywhere.

Commando squads of killer Autons in their dark overalls began to attack communications centres. Telephone exchanges, radio and TV transmitters, underground power cables, all exploded in flames under repeated blasts from the Auton weapons. Radios, TV screens and telephones went silent.

Completely cut off from each other, little groups of soldiers, policemen, Government officials, desperately tried to make sense of the situation, tried to find some way of combating the enemy. And all the while they eyed one another uneasily. No one knew when a familiar hand would drop away to reveal the wrist-gun of an Auton.

There were, of course, one or two successes. A group of quarrymen broke open their explosives hut and blew several Autons to pieces with blasting charges. Here and there tanks prowled the streets, shooting down or crushing the Autons in their path. Little groups of soldiers became tired of waiting for orders and for reinforcements that never came. Acting on their own initiative they raided their own armouries for what weapons they could find and fought desperate little street battles, turning bazookas, trench-mortars and anti-tank guns against the enemy.

UNIT H.Q. was under siege. The sleepy duty soldier who had opened the main doors that morning had been greeted by an energy-blast from a waiting Auton that missed him by inches. He had promptly slammed the doors shut again, and pressed the button that activated a second pair of reinforcing doors in heavy armour-plate. All over UNIT H.Q., emergency doors and shutters slammed down.

In his office the Brigadier had sent out desperate calls for help. Everywhere it was the same story. Chaos...

panic… confusion… Then, one by one, the outside 'phones went dead.

The Brigadier had told the Doctor of the situation as far as he knew it. The Doctor nodded gravely. 'Much as I feared,' he said. 'I'd hoped for a little more time…' And even as he listened, he had gone on working on the complicated electronic device. Now, waiting in his office, the Brigadier wondered if the thing would ever be ready. Not that it mattered, he thought gloomily. There was little they could do now. Maybe take a few of the enemy with them before the inevitable end. The internal 'phone, still powered by the emergency generator, suddenly buzzed. The Brigadier snatched it up. 'We're ready now,' said the Doctor's voice. The Brigadier slammed down the 'phone and ran to the laboratory.

He found Liz and the Doctor contemplating the completed device. Two army knapsacks rested on the bench. The first contained a jumble of electronic equipment, the second a portable power-pack. A long flex connected the first knapsack to the second. The Doctor was busily plugging what looked like a microphone, also on a long flex, into the pack containing the equipment.

The Brigadier looked at the contraption dubiously. 'Is that *it*?'

'Of course that's *it*,' said the Doctor. 'This first knapsack carries the device itself. The second, which will be carried by Miss Shaw, holds the power source.' He beamed proudly at his brain-child.

'And what's this?' said the Brigadier, indicating the microphone-like object. 'I thought we wanted to destroy them, not interview them.'

'This,' said the Doctor, 'is the… er, business end. A UHF

148

transmitter. The device is effective only at very short range, I'm afraid.'

'He means you practically have to shove it down their throats,' explained Liz.

The Brigadier looked unimpressed. 'Will it work?'

'We shan't know that till we try. Are you ready for the attack?'

'As ready as we'll ever be. I never thought I'd lead a force consisting of headquarters clerical staff, a female scientist and…' At a loss for words he waved his hand towards the Doctor.

'Cheer up, Brigadier,' said the Doctor. 'It's quality that counts, you know, not quantity. Shall we go?' He passed Liz the power-pack and shouldered the other himself.

A few moments later the Brigadier and his little force, loaded into two jeeps, were waiting in the UNIT garage. The Doctor was at the wheel of one jeep, accompanied by Liz and two soldiers. The Brigadier and the remaining soldiers were crammed into the other. The soldiers were heavily armed with a variety of curious weapons. The engines were already revving up. The Brigadier gave a signal and a soldier pressed the button to open the steel garage doors, and jumped in the back of the jeep. As soon as the doors began to open the Doctor gunned his jeep into a racing start and shot up the ramp. The Brigadier's jeep followed close behind. Energy bolts from waiting Autons whizzed round their heads, but the little jeeps weaved in and out of the attackers and disappeared out of sight.

Afterwards Liz could only remember that journey out of London as a kind of nightmare. By now the streets were empty, so there was no traffic to delay them. There was wreckage and devastation all around. Many buildings were now ablaze but there was no sound of fire engines speeding to the rescue. Fire stations had been one of the Auton's first targets, and by now most fire engines were destroyed.

They passed little groups of fleeing, terrified people. One or two of them shouted out warnings. The route they took went through side streets and back alleys, away from the shopping centres, away from the Autons. Occasionally Autons did appear and fired after them, often missing by inches. Once an Auton stepped directly in front of their jeep, wrist-gun raised. The Doctor put his foot down and smashed straight into it, sending it flying against the side of a building. Liz looked over her shoulder and saw to her horror that the Auton had lurched to its feet and was firing after them.

Soon, to her heartfelt relief, they were leaving the suburbs behind them, speeding down country lanes to the plastics factory where everything had begun, and where everything must be ended if there was to be any hope for mankind.

In the woods just outside the factory a solitary figure had been curled hidden in a ditch for hours. Unaware of all that had been happening in the cities, George Hibbert had been taking the advice given by the Doctor in the waxworks – to get away from Channing so that he could think. Gradually, in the peace and quiet of the forest, Hibbert's brain had cleared at last. The full horror of what he had become flooded over him. But at last he was himself again. At last he could think his own thoughts. And he knew what he must do. Stiffly he rose to his feet and began to walk back towards the factory.

Inside the factory itself Channing stood in silent

communion with the creature in the tank. Through the shared Nestene mind he was aware of all the destruction he had caused. Channing was pleased. Everything was going as it should. He was aware, too, that the Doctor and the Brigadier with their tiny force were on the way to attack him. He wondered idly what made these humans struggle so desperately to the last.

The factory was now almost empty of the killer Autons. They had been sent to do their deadly work around the country. Only a small group remained, to guard the creature in the tank. The creature that would soon emerge and take its rightful place as ruler. But Channing was not disturbed by the fact that there were so few Autons. He had made his arrangements. The factory was still well guarded.

A voice behind him said: 'Channing.' He turned. Hibbert was walking towards him, an iron crowbar in his hand. He said: 'Hibbert. There you are. I have been worried about you.'

A wave of hatred flooded over Hibbert at the sound of that familiar voice. He heard Channing say: 'You should not have gone away, Hibbert. It is safer for you to stay with me.'

Hibbert's voice was harsh. 'So that you can go on controlling my mind. Oh no, Channing. The Doctor was right. I can think, away from you.'

'You have spoken again to the Doctor?'

'He was at the waxworks. He knows what you're up to. He'll stop you.'

Channing was amused. 'He may know, Hibbert. But there is nothing he can do. Our invasion of your planet has already begun.'

Hibbert looked at him in loathing. 'Who are you? What

are you?'

Channing said: 'We are the Nestenes. We have been colonising other planets for a thousand million years. Now we have come to take Earth.'

'But what's going to happen to us – to *Man*?' The full horror of it suddenly came over Hibbert. 'You'll destroy us.'

Channing's voice was soothing. 'Not you, Hibbert. You are our ally. You have helped us.'

Hibbert said dully: 'And you... you're not human.'

'I am part of the whole, Hibbert. Nestenes have no individual existence. This body is merely a container, Hibbert. You should know that. You made me.'

And Channing smiled a terrible smile.

All the things which had been blocked from Hibbert's mind now came back to him. He remembered finding the green pulsating globe in the woods, the night of the first meteor shower. He remembered taking the globe back to the factory. He remembered staring as if hypnotised into its flashing green depths.

It had seemed as if the globe was talking, deep within his mind. It had told him of the other globes, and where to find them. It had told him how to design the new machinery, to order the parts, to assemble them himself. It had told him of the special plastics mix that had to be fed into the tanks, and how to attach the electrodes to the globe to transfer its energy.

Night after night Hibbert had worked, secretly in the deserted factory. Luckily, Ransome was on that trip to America. Then finally Hibbert had stood beside a bubbling tank of plastics mix, and connected the electrodes and thrown the switch. The globes had flashed and then died.

The tank of bubbling plastic seethed with life. A shape within it began to solidify, and dripping from its depths rose something in the shape of a man. The something that was now called Channing.

After that things became hazy in Hibbert's mind. He and Channing had made the Autons, and the Autons had made other Autons. All the time Channing's grip on his mind had grown stronger and stronger. Finally, he had had no thoughts of his own at all. He had become merely an extension of Channing's will. But all that was over now. He had broken free.

Suddenly Hibbert gestured to the giant plastic coffin with his crowbar. 'And that thing in there?'

'That is our real form, Hibbert. The form we once had on our own planet, before we shook off the body and became pure mind. We created human forms for ourselves to help begin our invasion. But once the planet is ours, we shall re-create the form that was once our own.' Channing laughed, looking proudly at the tank. 'In there is the repository of all the Nestene consciousness. Would you like to see it, Hibbert?' Again Channing laughed, and the thing within the plastic tank bubbled and seethed as though sharing in his mirth.

Hibbert snatched at one central thought. 'Then if you exist as one, you can die as one!'

He leaped towards the tank, crowbar raised. But before he could reach it an Auton stepped from the shadows and blasted him from existence. At a sign from Channing the Auton blasted at Hibbert's body with its energy-gun until, like Ransome before him, he had totally disappeared.

Channing suddenly stiffened. Through the eyes of an Auton posted in the woods near the factory, he saw the

153

UNIT jeeps flashing by. Channing wondered again at this stupid insistence of the humans on fighting to the very last minute. He left the Restricted Area to prepare to meet them.

Jolting across the woodlands between the trees, the Brigadier's little force had driven the jeeps to the very edge of the wire fence surrounding the factory. Swiftly and efficiently two soldiers cut a gap in the fencing. The Brigadier went through first, followed by the Doctor and Liz, carrying the two linked packs. The handful of soldiers followed after them. They moved swiftly and silently to the factory buildings, and up to a small back door. It was locked. At a nod from the Brigadier one of his men blew it open. The little group moved through the shattered door and into the factory itself.

They looked round in amazement. The place was totally deserted now, and the strange alien machines were silent, their work for the moment over.

'Where's everybody gone?' said Liz uneasily.

'They're here – somewhere,' said the Doctor. 'That's the place we want.' He pointed towards the Restricted Area. But before they could take another step, armed men appeared from hiding and sprang up all round them. Liz was delighted to see they wore the uniform of the Regular Army.

'You've got some reinforcements after all, Brigadier,' she said.

The Doctor glanced around. 'I don't think so, Liz,' he said gently. 'Those guns are pointed at us.'

To her utter amazement Liz saw that he was right. The young Captain in charge of the soldiers had drawn his

154

revolver and was covering the Brigadier.

'Brigadier, you and your men are under arrest. Please lay down your arms immediately.'

From the door of the Restricted Area, Channing watched. It had amused him to have his factory guarded with human soldiers.

The Brigadier could scarcely believe his ears. 'What the blazes do you think you're up to, man?' he snapped. 'Don't you realise that we're being invaded, and this place is the centre of it all? Put down that gun and give me some help.'

Confidently the Brigadier strode towards the young officer. The Captain raised his revolver. 'I'm sorry, sir, but I have my orders. I'll shoot if you force me to. Now order your men to lay down their arms, or my men will fire.'

'Then they'll have to shoot, Captain.' The Brigadier's voice was calm. 'We came here to do a job and we're going to do it. Now are you really going to open fire on a fellow officer? Or are you going to be sensible and place yourself under my command?'

Liz glanced at the Doctor. She nodded towards the weapon they carried, but the Doctor shook his head. It might or might not work against the Autons, but against human soldiers it was useless.

Liz looked at the young Captain, wondering what he would do. It was obvious that he had not expected things to go this far.

The Brigadier said: 'Well? Make your mind up. Because I assure you I'm going in there.' He nodded towards the Restricted Area. Concealed behind the doorway, Channing watched impatiently. By now the Brigadier should have surrendered, since he was so hopelessly outnumbered. Again this tiresome human insistence on continued resistance. Were they too stupid to give up? Channing wondered.

There was an edge of panic in the Captain's voice. He stubbornly repeated: 'I have my orders.' The Brigadier took another step forward.

Suddenly the Doctor's voice broke the tense silence. 'I'm no expert in military matters, but surely the Brigadier outranks you. Shouldn't you obey his orders now?' For a moment it looked as if the Captain would give way. He lowered his revolver. Then someone stepped from the shadows. It was, or rather it seemed to be, General Scobie. Liz felt the Doctor tense with excitement beside her. He gave her a warning tap on the elbow and began to edge towards the General. Liz followed with the power-pack.

The Captain turned thankfully to the figure of General Scobie, relieved to be free of his terrible responsibility.

'For the last time, Brigadier, will you surrender, or shall I order my men to shoot you down?' The General's voice was harsh and threatening. Not a bit like the real Scobie, thought Liz. But real enough to convince those soldiers.

By now Liz and the Doctor had edged their way round the group and were standing close to Scobie.

The Brigadier said: 'Now, listen to me, Captain, this is not the real General Scobie.'

'I'm sorry, sir, but it certainly is,' said the Captain. 'I've served on the General's staff. I know him well.'

'Perhaps I can settle the argument,' said the Doctor. 'Would you care to say a few words into this?' He held the microphone-like object close to Scobie's face and snapped: 'Switch on, Liz!'

Liz reached inside the power-pack and turned on the controls.

Scobie said: 'What is this nonsense…?' He clasped his hands to his face and fell writhing to the ground. His body became still.

The Captain turned on the Doctor. 'You've killed him!'

'Oh, I don't think so,' said the Doctor. 'You see, he was never really alive.' He knelt by Scobie's body and turned it over. The face had become blank, lumpy, featureless. Like that of an Auton.

(Far away in London the real General Scobie suddenly awoke, and was astonished to find himself alone in the Replica Room of the waxworks.)

The Captain gazed at Scobie's face in horrified unbelief.

'Well,' snapped the Brigadier, 'now will you place your men under my orders?'

The last vestige of doubt disappeared from the Captain's mind. 'Yes, sir,' he said.

Then from inside the Restricted Area marched a line of Autons.

'Take cover!' yelled the Brigadier. UNIT men and Regulars found what cover they could behind the factory machinery. The Auton hands dropped down on their hinges, and energy-bolts blazed from their guns. The Brigadier and his soldiers did their best to hold the advancing Autons. The bullets from the Regulars' rifles had little or no effect. But the Brigadier had equipped his men with sub-machine-guns and grenades, and the UNIT armoury had even managed to produce one anti-tank rifle. The heavier weapons did have some effect. As the soldiers returned the Autons' fire, the din in the little factory was deafening. Liz watched horrified as several soldiers, struck by sizzling energy-bolts, were hurled clear across the room to collapse like empty sacks against the walls. From the corner where she and the Doctor were hiding, she saw Autons cut to pieces by machine-gun bullets, and blown to pieces by grenades. An Auton arm blown clear from the body continued to lash wildly round the room, spitting energy-bolts like a demented snake.

Liz became aware that the Autons were gaining. Their line was moving ever closer to the spot where she and the Doctor were hiding. She tugged at the Doctor's sleeve. Surely they ought to fall back too? The Doctor shook his head. He gestured to Liz to be ready with the power-pack. Then, quite deliberately, the Doctor rose to his feet. He stepped full in the path of an advancing Auton and thrust the transmitter near its face. Without waiting to be told, Liz switched on the power-pack. The Auton suddenly slumped, collapsing almost on top of them.

Huddled behind the shelter of the Auton's body, Liz and the Doctor waited, as the line of other Autons swept over and past them. Liz's nose was no more than an inch from the Auton's outstretched arm. She looked at the big hand – it was the left one, the one without the gun – and shuddered at the blunt fingers with no fingernails. Then the Doctor tugged her to her feet.

'We've done it, Liz,' he whispered exultantly, 'we're behind the enemy lines.' With the battle raging behind them, Liz and the Doctor ran for the now unguarded door to the Restricted Area.

Once they were inside, both stopped in amazement. The room seemed to be empty. It was dominated by the vast coffin-shaped tank. Inside the tank something enormous heaved, and seethed and bubbled.

Liz looked up at the Doctor. 'There's something alive in there,' she said. 'Oh yes,' said the Doctor mildly. 'I rather thought there would be, you know. It was the logical next step. You remember, poor Ransome told us about it.' The Doctor sounded pleased to have his theories confirmed. To her amazement Liz saw that his face showed not fear, but a sort of detached scientific curiosity.

'Now, I wonder...' said the Doctor, and he walked round the tank as if contemplating a swim in it.

'Doctor, you're not going in there,' said Liz, as the Doctor dragged over a crate to stand on.

'Someone's got to, you know. Our friend in there is the key to everything.'

'Quite right, Doctor. But your discovery has come too late.' Channing stepped from behind the tank, and stood facing them.

'Oh, I don't know,' said the Doctor. 'There's a saying on this planet that it's never too late.'

Channing looked at the Doctor. 'You speak as if you are not one of the humans.'

'As a matter of fact, I'm not.'

'I thought as much when you first came here. Your mind has a different feel to these humans. There are depths in it I cannot reach.'

The Doctor said: 'Like you, I am not of this planet. But I didn't come here of my own choice. Why did you come?'

'We are Nestenes. Our purpose is conquest – always. We must spread the Nestene mind, the Nestene consciousness throughout all the galaxies.'

'We?' asked the Doctor keenly. 'You speak for all your people?'

'I am all my people,' said Channing simply. 'We are the Nestenes. We are all one.'

'A collective brain, a collective nervous system, is that

159

it? And as far as Earth is concerned, all housed in that life form in the tank?'

'Exactly so!' said Channing. His voice rose to an exultant shout. 'Would you like to look upon the true form of the Nestenes, Doctor – before you die?'

The fluid in the tank heaved and bubbled in a final convulsion. The whole side of the tank shattered open, as the Doctor and Liz leaped back.

Standing towering over them was the most nightmarish creature Liz had ever seen. A huge, many-tentacled monster something between spider, crab and octopus. The nutrient fluids from the tank were still streaming down its sides. At the front of its glistening body a single huge eye glared at them, blazing with alien intelligence and hatred.

The Doctor stood peering up at it with an expression of fascinated interest. 'Remarkable,' he said. 'Quite remarkable.' Then he shouted: 'Now, Liz!'

But just as he spoke the Nestene monster lashed out with one of its many tentacles and began to drag the Doctor towards it. Liz switched on the power-pack. Nothing happened.

'Now, Liz! Now!' the Doctor shouted urgently. Again Liz flicked the controls, and again there was no result. Liz realised that when the monster grabbed the Doctor, the lead connecting the Doctor's machine to her pack had been pulled out.

The monster was dragging the Doctor closer and closer. He struggled frantically as a second slimy tentacle wrapped itself round his throat, beginning to throttle him. Liz ducked under the creature, scrabbling for the other end of the lead. She grabbed it and began to plug it in. Angrily, yet another tentacle wrapped round *her*, but with a final desperate effort

Liz managed to jam the lead into its socket.

Immediately, there was a hum of power from the Doctor's machine. As Liz turned the power up to its highest notch the Doctor shoved the microphone-shaped transmitter up to the single blazing eye. Immediately, the monster gave a single agonised howl that seemed to shatter Liz's eardrums. The tentacles holding Liz and the Doctor lost their power and they fell to the ground.

Then, as they watched, the hideous creation that had housed the Nestene mind began to blur and dissolve. It seemed to melt away before them like a wax model in a blast of fierce heat.

Finally there was nothing left but a sort of vast spreading puddle of thick, slimy liquid. For a moment that single eye remained floating in the puddle, glaring its hatred at them to the last. Then it, too, dissolved. The Nestene was dead.

Liz and the Doctor picked themselves up. The Doctor saw Channing, face downwards where he had fallen. He turned the body over. Like Scobie's Replica before him, Channing now had the crude blank features of an Auton. The Doctor looked up. 'Nothing to be frightened of, my dear,' he said gently. 'It's only a waxwork.'

A minute or two before, as Liz was struggling to reconnect the Doctor's machine to the power-pack, Brigadier Alastair Lethbridge-Stewart had resigned himself to the end of a not-inglorious military career. He and his men had fought a gallant rearguard action across the factory, many being blasted to extinction by Nestene energy-bolts in the process. The few left alive were now trapped in an angle of the factory wall, under a deadly crossfire from two groups of advancing Autons. The Brigadier cut an advancing Auton in two with a savage burst from his sub-machine-gun. The gun emptied itself, and the Brigadier automatically reached for another magazine from his belt. But the belt was empty. Another Auton appeared in front of the Brigadier, its wrist-gun aimed at point-blank range. The Brigadier gazed into the nozzle of the gun, waiting for the final blast. Then, to his amazement, the outstretched arm seemed to wilt before his eyes. It drooped, and the Auton crashed to the floor. All around, the other Autons were collapsing too.

Suddenly there was silence. Powder smoke drifted in low clouds through the still air of the factory. The Brigadier and his few remaining men looked at each other in astonishment, scarcely able to believe that they were still alive. A voice cut through the silence. 'Brigadier! Where are you, Brigadier!' came the Doctor's voice impatiently. 'Are you all right?' The Brigadier ran for the Restricted Area.

Liz and the Doctor waited in the doorway. Behind them the Brigadier could see some kind of nasty oozy mess spreading over the floor. Tired but happy, the Doctor surveyed the scene. Behind him was the shattered tank, the dissolved monster and the remains of Channing.

In front of him the bullet-shattered factory, the collapsed Autons, and the soldiers who had died holding them back.

'Glad to see you're all right, Doctor, Miss Shaw,' said the Brigadier.

'I'm not sure if I am yet,' said Liz shakily.

The Doctor put a comforting arm round her shoulders. 'I think we've won, Liz,' he said gently. 'But the price has been very high.'

It wasn't until they were safely back at UNIT H.Q. that they realised it was really all over. When the Nestene monster had died at the plastics factory, Autons all over the country had become instantly lifeless, as harmless as the waxworks they resembled. Much damage had been done, and many lives lost. But gradually the country was pulling itself together again, and soon a return to normal life would begin.

In the UNIT laboratory the returned warriors were celebrating in mugs of strong, sweet army tea. Proudly the Doctor was explaining the workings of his machine.

'Basically, it's a sort of ECT machine – electro-convulsive therapy. Only much more powerful. You see, the Nestenes were held together and animated by that one central brain. In a sense they were all literally part of one vast creature. A creature that could split itself up, put fractions of its consciousness into different forms. It put just a tiny bit of itself into the Autons. Just enough so that they could move and think, in the simplest possible way. They weren't really alive at all.'

Liz shivered. 'They were alive enough for me!'

The Doctor took a swig of his tea and went on. 'It put a bit more of itself into the Replicas. They could pick up and reproduce the pattern of a human brain, and give quite a good imitation of a human being.'

'What about this fellow Channing?' asked the Brigadier.

The Doctor rubbed his chin. 'I think it put a tremendous amount of itself into Channing. He was the advance guard. He could think, and plan. I think he could even feel, in a way, though his emotions weren't really like ours.'

'And that creature in the factory?' Liz asked.

'Well, since the Nestenes are really just one creature,' the Doctor explained, 'I suppose it was more comfortable for them to have the part of them that was here all in one body. When Channing really got organised at the factory he set about creating a suitable receptacle. And as soon as it was ready they transferred all of themselves, or rather all of itself, all its vital energy, from the meteorite state into that one collective brain.'

'Putting all their eggs into one basket?' said the Brigadier.

'Just so,' said the Doctor. 'And by giving the creature a kind of brain-storm, you might say I kicked over the basket.'

'You said "the part of them that was here", Doctor,' said Liz. 'You mean there's more of it?'

'Oh, I should think so,' said the Doctor cheerfully. 'I don't suppose the Nestene brain risked all of itself on this planet.'

The Brigadier said: 'Then they might try again?'

The Doctor looked thoughtful. 'It's possible. But they've had a pretty severe setback. And since they seem to communicate by telepathy the rest of the Nestene brain will know how badly they were defeated here.'

Liz said practically: 'Do they know how limited the range of UHF waves are? You practically have to stand on their toes for that thing to work.'

The Doctor nodded. 'That is something I hope they haven't learned.'

The Brigadier said: 'Doctor, if the Nestenes do decide to launch a second attack, can we rely on your help again?'

The Doctor gave him a quizzical look. 'Do I take it that you're satisfied that I'm not an impostor?'

'Oh, I think so,' said the Brigadier. 'Two things combined to convince me, actually.'

'Oh, yes?' said the Doctor curiously.

'The brilliance of your scientific results was one,' said the Brigadier.

'And the other?' said the Doctor, with a modest smile.

'Your uniquely, aggravating temperament,' the Brigadier said crisply. 'There couldn't be two like you anywhere, Doctor. Your face may have changed, but not your character!'

For a moment the Doctor looked offended, then he caught Liz's eye and grinned.

The Brigadier went on: 'I am prepared to offer you the post of UNIT's Scientific Adviser – since Miss Shaw here doesn't seem to want it. What do you say?'

The Doctor looked thoughtful. 'I really think we ought to discuss terms first, old chap.'

'Terms?' said the Brigadier. Liz could tell from his voice that he thought the honour of working for UNIT should be reward enough.

'Terms?' the Brigadier said again. 'Well, I think you'll find the salary adequate.'

'My dear chap, I don't want money,' said the Doctor indignantly. 'Got no use for the stuff.'

The Brigadier looked puzzled. 'Then what do you want?'

'Facilities to repair the TARDIS! Equipment, a laboratory, somewhere to sleep. Oh, and I insist that Miss Shaw stays on here to help me.'

He looked appealingly at Liz. So did the Brigadier.

'Well, Miss Shaw?' he said.

Liz took a deep breath and then nodded. 'I must be raving mad,' she said. 'But all right. If you really want me to.'

The Brigadier said: 'There you are, then, Doctor.

Anything else?'

'Good heavens, yes! Do you realise I'm stranded here with nothing more than I stand up in?' The Doctor looked guilty. 'Come to think of it, most of that isn't really mine. Oh dear, and there's that car, too.' He looked appealingly at the Brigadier. 'You know, I really took to that car. It's got character.'

'No, Doctor,' said the Brigadier firmly. 'The car must go back to its owner.'

The Doctor sighed. 'Yes, yes, I suppose it must. But there's no reason why you shouldn't find me another one like it, is there?'

The Brigadier looked as if he was about to explode when the Doctor said gently: 'It would help to persuade me to stay, you know.'

'Oh, very well,' growled the Brigadier.

Liz couldn't help smiling at the Doctor's air of childlike pleasure.

'Oh good,' he said happily. 'When can I go out and choose it?'

'Not just yet,' said the Brigadier patiently. 'At the moment you have no official existence, Doctor. I must fix you up with a full set of papers first.' He turned to go, and then stopped. 'By the way, Doctor, I've just realised. I don't even know your name.'

The Doctor looked from the Brigadier to Liz Shaw. All in all he was quite looking forward to his stay on Earth. Naturally, he wouldn't be there for long. In spite of the Time Lords he'd soon manage to get the TARDIS working and be off on his travels. For instance, he could try reversing the polarity of the neutron flow in the dematerialisation circuit…

He was brought out of his daydream by the Brigadier's voice. 'Well, Doctor?'

Ah yes, a name… he thought. Just for the time he was here. No question of telling them his real name, of course. Time Lord names have an almost mystic importance, and are usually kept closely-guarded secrets. Anyway, they'd never be able to pronounce it. A name… thought the Doctor. Something simple, dignified and modest. He didn't want to draw attention to himself. The Doctor's eyes brightened. He'd got it – the very thing! He turned to the waiting Brigadier.

'Smith,' said the Doctor decisively. 'Doctor John Smith!'

About the Authors

Terrance Dicks

Born in East Ham in London in 1935, Terrance Dicks worked in the advertising industry after leaving university before moving into television as a writer. He worked together with Malcolm Hulke on scripts for *The Avengers* as well as other series before becoming Assistant and later full Script Editor of *Doctor Who* from 1968.

Working closely with friend and series Producer Barry Letts, Dicks worked on the entirety of the Third Doctor Jon Pertwee's era of the programme, and returned as a writer – scripting Tom Baker's first story as the Fourth Doctor: 'Robot'. He left *Doctor Who* to work as first Script Editor and then Producer on the BBC's prestigious Classic Serials, and to pursue his writing career on screen and in print. His later scriptwriting credits on *Doctor Who* included the twentieth-anniversary story 'The Five Doctors'.

Terrance Dicks novelised many of the original *Doctor Who* stories for Target, and discovered a liking and talent for prose fiction. He has written extensively for children, creating such memorable series and characters as T.R. Bear and the Baker Street Irregulars, as well as continuing to write original *Doctor Who* novels for BBC Books.

Robert Holmes

Robert Holmes served with distinction in the army and also in the police before becoming a journalist. He also started to write for television series, including *Emergency Ward 10*.

After rewriting his proposed *Doctor Who* story 'The Space Trap' as 'The Krotons' in 1969, Holmes went on to become one of the programme's most prolific writers. He took over from Terrance Dicks as Script Editor of *Doctor Who* in 1974, working mainly with producer Philip Hinchcliffe during one of the programme's most successful periods at the start of the Fourth Doctor's era. During this time he extensively revised or reworked many of the scripts for the programme and wrote 'Pyramids of Mars' under the pseudonym Stephen Harris.

Holmes wrote the introductory stories for both the Third Doctor ('Spearhead from Space') and the Master ('Terror of the Autons'). Several of his scripts are considered amongst the absolute best ever in *Doctor Who* – including 'The Talons of Weng-Chiang' and the Fifth Doctor's final story, 'The Caves of Androzani'. In 'The Deadly Assassin', Holmes established a background and society for the Time Lords that has endured to this day.

Robert Holmes wrote for many other series including *Doomwatch*, *Spy Trap*, *Dixon of Dock Green*, *Blake's 7*, and was Story Editor on *Armchair Theatre*. He also adapted David Wiltshire's book *Child of the Vodyanoi* for television, retitling it *The Nightmare Man*.

Robert Holmes died in 1986, while working on the final episodes of the *Doctor Who* story 'The Trial of a Time Lord'.

Doctor Who and the Auton Invasion
Between the Lines

Doctor Who and Terrance Dicks had a busy year in 1974. The conclusion of the eleventh season in June, script edited by Dicks, saw the departure of Jon Pertwee's Third Doctor and his replacement by Tom Baker. A few days before Baker's debut story, 'Robot' (written by Dicks), began in December, the Doctor made his West End debut in *Seven Keys to Doomsday* – also scripted by Dicks. And the Target division of Universal-Tandem Publishing followed its republication of three 1960s novelisations the previous year with the first two new titles on Thursday 17 January, one by Malcolm Hulke, the other by Terrance Dicks.

Doctor Who and the Auton Invasion and *Doctor Who and the Cave Monsters* retold the first two adventures of the Third Doctor, 'Spearhead from Space' and 'Doctor Who and the Silurians', which had been broadcast four years earlier, between 3 January and 14 March 1970. Malcolm Hulke novelised his own scripts, but Terrance Dicks was adapting the work of Robert Holmes, which he had script edited. The interior illustrations (used in this edition) were by Chris Achilleos, who also drew the cover artwork.

This new edition re-presents that 1974 publication. While a few minor errors or inconsistencies have been corrected, no attempt has been made to update or modernise the text – this is *Doctor Who and the Auton Invasion* as originally written and published. This means that the novel

171

retains certain stylistic and editorial practices that were current in 1973 (when the book was written and prepared for publication) but which have since adapted or changed.

Most obviously, measurements are given in the then-standard imperial system of weights and measures: a yard is equivalent to 0.9144 metres; three feet make a yard, and a foot is 30 centimetres; twelve inches make a foot, and an inch is 25.4 millimetres.

Although he stuck very faithfully to the narrative of the television episodes, Terrance Dicks took the opportunity to greatly extend the characterisation, expanding certain scenes and filling in background detail for several of the story's protagonists. Notably, he includes a prelude, adapted from scenes featured at the conclusion of 'The War Games', Patrick Troughton's last serial as the Second Doctor. It had been five years since this story had been seen on UK television, so it was important to give younger readers a succinct explanation of exactly why the Doctor spends the first half of the story in a hospital bed, unrecognised by the only man he knows. This recap of the Doctor's trial replaces televised scenes showing staff at a UNIT tracking station monitoring the incoming 'meteorites'.

The coincidence of the Doctor's arrival in the midst of this meteorite shower is strengthened by having poacher Sam Seeley witness not just the landing of the Nestene spheres but also the materialisation of the TARDIS. A scene in which Seeley is stopped by a UNIT patrol in Episode 1 is replaced with Seeley escaping discovery by a nervous soldier in the third chapter. Dicks adds colour to the relationship between Seeley and his wife in Chapter 3, and gives an insight into the poacher's dreams of fame and fortune in Chapter 5. Similarly, he gives the senior hospital staff a range of fearsome reputations and rivalries barely glimpsed on screen. At the plastics factory, Harry Ransome (John Ransome on TV) and George Hibbert's partnership is more thoroughly explored, with a description added of the electronic talking doll, even giving it a few lines sadly denied to its television counterpart. And readers get a glimpse of Hibbert's discovery of the first Nestene sphere and his subsequent manufacture of – and domination by – Channing. Mullins the hospital porter, General Scobie and even the shortlived police officer who dies in the first wave of Auton attacks in Chapter 10 are each given extra moments – aghast at the effects of a call to the press, yearning for a straightforward cavalry charge, longing for a holiday – that could not be incorporated into the TV episodes.

There are many small changes to the action, too. The opening moments of Episode 2 are revised slightly to form the cliffhanger ending to Chapter 4, and the soldiers' discovery of an intact Nestene sphere in Chapter 6 is extended so Captain Munro can gallantly share the honour with his corporal. Forbes's grisly fate, too, is given more detail – on screen, the unnamed corporal is simply forced off the road by an Auton. Chapter 7 bypasses a brief scene in which the Doctor berates the concierge on duty at UNIT's main gate, in favour of an internal phone call to the Brigadier. Although the Brigadier doesn't discover how the Doctor located UNIT's top secret base in print, readers have already seen the Doctor consult his TARDIS detector during the previous chapter; on screen, the Doctor answers the Brigadier's question and shows him the detector. The Doctor's claim to have passed his driving test 'on the Mars to Venus route' is new to the novel, although it fits well with the Third Doctor's regular boasts and anecdotes in other

TV stories. On his visit to Madame Tussaud's, the Doctor's plan to arrest the waxworks and take them back to UNIT for testing is invented for the book.

The launch of the Nestene assault is greatly extended. On television, the conditions of early morning location filming restricted the attack's representation to the sound of a window smashing, a policeman and several pedestrians and cyclists being shot down, and a group of Autons progressing eerily down a now-deserted street, while the Brigadier reports Autons coming to life all over the country. In print, Terrance Dicks is able to add waves of attacks across London, the police deluged with calls, televised public warnings, and the declaration of martial law. He shows the effects of the placement of Auton duplicates in positions of authority, and describes how the Replicas begin to be uncovered. UNIT's operation at Auto Plastics is also revised to allow a lengthier standoff with the Regular Army troops, before General Scobie's duplicate is destroyed. Once inside the Restricted Area, Dicks has the Doctor contemplate climbing into the Nestene tank, before Channing's arrival brings events back in sync with the TV original. On screen, Liz is slower to realise that the power lead has detached from the Doctor's device, and it is only the Doctor who is grabbed by the Nestene's tentacles.

The final paragraphs of *Doctor Who and the Auton Invasion* also introduce a phrase heard in full just once on television by that time, but which would return in numerous future novelisations and become a famous part of the *Doctor Who* mythos. Contemplating how he might repair the TARDIS, the Doctor wonders for the first time what might happen if he reversed the polarity of the neutron flow...

Here are details of other exciting Doctor Who *titles from BBC Books:*

DOCTOR WHO AND THE DALEKS
David Whitaker   £4.99
ISBN 978 1 849 90195 6   **A First Doctor adventure**

With a new introduction by **NEIL GAIMAN**

'The voice was all on one level, without any expression at all, a dull monotone that still managed to convey a terrible sense of evil...'

The mysterious Doctor and his granddaughter Susan are joined by unwilling adventurers Ian Chesterton and Barbara Wright in an epic struggle for survival on an alien planet.

In a vast metal city they discover the survivors of a terrible nuclear war – the Daleks. Held captive in the deepest levels of the city, can the Doctor and his new companions stop the Daleks' plan to totally exterminate their mortal enemies, the peace-loving Thals? More importantly, even if they can escape from the Daleks, will Ian and Barbara ever see their home planet Earth again?

This novel is based on the second Doctor Who *story, which was originally broadcast from 21 December 1963 to 1 February 1964. This was the first ever* Doctor Who *novel, first published in 1964.*

DOCTOR WHO AND THE CRUSADERS
David Whitaker £4.99
ISBN 978 1 849 90190 1 **A First Doctor adventure**

With a new introduction by **CHARLIE HIGSON**

'I admire bravery, sir. And bravery and courage are clearly in you in full measure. Unfortunately, you have no brains at all. I despise fools.'

Arriving in the Holy Land in the middle of the Third Crusade, the Doctor and his companions run straight into trouble. The Doctor and Vicki befriend Richard the Lionheart, but must survive the cut-throat politics of the English court. Even with the king on their side, they find they have made powerful enemies.

Looking for Barbara, Ian is ambushed – staked out in the sand and daubed with honey so that the ants will eat him. With Ian unable to help, Barbara is captured by the cruel warlord El Akir. Even if Ian escapes and rescues her, will they ever see the Doctor, Vicki and the TARDIS again?

This novel is based on a Doctor Who *story which was originally broadcast from 27 March to 17 April 1965, featuring the First Doctor as played by William Hartnell, and his companions Ian, Barbara and Vicki.*

DOCTOR WHO AND THE CYBERMEN
Gerry Davis £4.99
ISBN 978 1 849 90191 8   **A Second Doctor adventure**

With a new introduction by **GARETH ROBERTS**

'There are some corners of the universe which have bred the most terrible things. Things which are against everything we have ever believed in. They must be fought. To the death.'

In 2070, the Earth's weather is controlled from a base on the moon. But when the Doctor and his friends arrive, all is not well. They discover unexplained drops of air pressure, minor problems with the weather control systems, and an outbreak of a mysterious plague.

With Jamie injured, and members of the crew going missing, the Doctor realises that the moonbase is under attack. Some malevolent force is infecting the crew and sabotaging the systems as a prelude to an invasion of Earth. And the Doctor thinks he knows who is behind it: the Cybermen.

This novel is based on 'The Moonbase', a Doctor Who story which was originally broadcast from 11 February to 4 March 1967, featuring the Second Doctor as played by Patrick Troughton, and his companions Polly, Ben and Jamie.

DOCTOR WHO AND THE ABOMINABLE SNOWMEN
Terrance Dicks £4.99
ISBN 978 1 849 90192 5 **A Second Doctor adventure**

With a new introduction by **STEPHEN BAXTER**

'Light flooded into the tunnel, silhouetting the enormous shaggy figure in the cave mouth. With a blood-curdling roar, claws outstretched, it bore down on Jamie.'

The Doctor has been to Det-Sen Monastery before, and expects the welcome of a lifetime. But the monastery is a very different place from when the Doctor last came. Fearing an attack at any moment by the legendary Yeti, the monks are prepared to defend themselves, and see the Doctor as a threat.

The Doctor and his friends join forces with Travers, an English explorer out to prove the existence of the elusive abominable snowmen. But they soon discover that these Yeti are not the timid animals that Travers seeks. They are the unstoppable servants of an alien Intelligence.

This novel is based on a Doctor Who *story which was originally broadcast from 30 September to 4 November 1967, featuring the Second Doctor as played by Patrick Troughton, and his companions Jamie and Victoria.*

DOCTOR WHO AND THE CAVE MONSTERS
Malcolm Hulke £4.99
ISBN 978 1 849 90194 9 **A Third Doctor adventure**

With a new introduction by **TERRANCE DICKS**

'Okdel looked across the valley to see the tip of the sun as it sank below the horizon. It was the last time he was to see the sun for a hundred million years.'

UNIT are called in to investigate security at a secret research centre buried under Wenley Moor. Unknown to the Doctor and his colleagues, the work at the centre has woken a group of Silurians – intelligent reptiles that used to be the dominant life form on Earth in prehistoric times.

Now they have woken, the Silurians are appalled to find 'their' planet populated by upstart apes. The Doctor hopes to negotiate a peace deal, but there are those on both sides who cannot bear the thought of humans and Silurians living together. As UNIT soldiers enters the cave systems, and the Silurians unleash a deadly plague that could wipe out the human race, the battle for planet Earth begins.

This novel is based on 'The Silurians', a Doctor Who *story which was originally broadcast from 31 January to 14 March 1970, featuring the Third Doctor as played by Jon Pertwee, with his companion Liz Shaw and the UNIT organisation commanded by Brigadier Lethbridge-Stewart.*